Books by Ed Dunlop

The Terrestria Chronicles
The Sword, the Ring, and the Parchment
The Quest for Seven Castles
The Search for Everyman
The Crown of Kuros
The Dragon's Egg
The Golden Lamps
The Great War

Tales from Terrestria
The Quest for Thunder Mountain
The Golden Dagger
The Return of the Dagger
The Isle of Dragons

Jed Cartwright Adventure Series
The Midnight Escape
The Lost Gold Mine
The Comanche Raiders
The Lighthouse Mystery
The Desperate Slave
The Midnight Rustlers

The Young Refugees Series
Escape to Liechtenstein
The Search for the Silver Eagle
The Incredible Rescues

Sherlock Jones Detective Series
Sherlock Jones and the Assassination Plot
Sherlock Jones and the Willoughby Bank Robbery
Sherlock Jones and the Missing Diamond
Sherlock Jones and the Phantom Airplane
Sherlock Jones and the Hidden Coins
Sherlock Jones and the Odyssey Mystery

The 1,000-Mile Journey

TALES FROM TERRESTRIA:

BOOK FOUR

*An allegory
by Ed Dunlop*

CROSS & CROWN
PUBLISHING
RINGGOLD, GEORGIA

www.talesofcastles.com
Cover Art by Rebecca Douglas

The Isle of Dragons: an allegory / by Ed Dunlop.
Dunlop, Ed.
[Ringgold, Ga.] : Cross and Crown Publishing, c2009
201 p. ; 22 cm.
Tales from Terrestria Bk. 4
Dewey Call # 813.54
ISBN 978-0-9817728-9-9

0-9817728-9-7

When sixteen-year-old Joel of Seawell attends the Dragon Tournaments,
he learns the terrifying secret of the Isle of Dragons. Taken captive
by slave traders, he despairs of ever again seeing his home.

Dunlop, Ed.
Middle ages juvenile fiction.
Christian life juvenile fiction.
Allegories.
Fantasy

Printed and bound in the United States of America

That the hearts
of young people
and their parents
would be drawn together.

*He that walketh with wise men
shall be wise: but a companion of fools
shall be destroyed.*

– Proverbs 13:20

Chapter One

The wind hummed in the rigging as the small fishing vessel bounded eagerly through the waves, proudly lifting her bow to meet each crest, briskly surging forward, and then dropping her bow to glide smoothly down into the trough. The single broadcloth sail, stark white against the darkness of the afternoon, stood taut and full against a brisk westerly wind.

Although the cog was a simple, single-masted ship of a mere thirty-foot length, there was a striking elegance about her. She carried herself with a regal bearing, almost a suggestion of nobility or even royalty, as if she did not see herself as a mere fishing vessel. Indeed, her given name was *Princess*.

Sixteen-year-old Joel stood amidships, silent and tight-lipped, momentarily studying the billowing sail as it strained and snapped. The swish of the bow as it sliced through the surging gray-blue waters, the humming of the rigging and the creaking of the mast—these were familiar sounds to the youth. He was at home with the violent pitching and rolling of the hull, the smell of fish and salt air, and the salt spray that splashed over the gunwales from time to time. The son of a fisherman, from a long line of fishermen, the tall, slender youth was very much a man of the sea.

"Pa," he said, addressing the leather-faced figure at the tiller but never taking his eyes from the sail, "isn't there some way to get any more speed out of her?"

"The *Princess* is giving her very best, Son," the stocky fisherman replied, glancing upward at the billowing sail himself. "A man can't ask more than that, can he?"

Joel turned and gazed aft across the vast expanse of surging gray water. Fear tightened in his chest like a cold fist gripping his heart. His hands trembled and he thrust them inside his greatcoat to conceal his nervousness. He took a deep breath to calm his racing heart. "They're still gaining on us, Pa."

His father nodded without taking his eyes from the waves. There was no need to turn for another look astern; he already knew the terror that pursued them. "Perhaps we should send another petition to King Emmanuel," he suggested.

Joel looked aft for several long moments and then turned to an older man who stood in the bow with a brass spyglass to his eye. "Papa Wynn, is there a chance we can outrun them?"

The old man didn't answer. He continued to gaze through the telescope.

The boy licked his lips nervously. "Papa Wynn—"

"I heard you, Joel," Wynn said, not unkindly. He lowered the spyglass and looked the boy in the eye. "The *Princess* is fast for a cog, lad, but she won't outrun the caravels. As you can see, they have far more sail area and longer, faster hulls. Unless His Majesty answers our petitions and intervenes, they'll be upon us in less than a quarter hour."

Joel took a deep breath and then let it out slowly. "What are we going to do?"

The two men looked at each other as if neither wanted to address the question. The *Princess* bounded forward eagerly like a dolphin, or, more accurately, like a bluefish trying desperately to outrun a shark. The wind gusted and howled, slicing the tops off the waves and hurling them across the open hull as cold, wet spray.

Two furlongs astern, a pair of tall, three-masted caravels bounded after the little cog like barracudas in pursuit of prey. Side by side, one ship slightly ahead of the other, they ran full sail before the wind. Even at that distance, the three fishermen aboard the *Princess* could see sword-brandishing crewmen lining the forward rail as the chase continued. "They've been pursuing us for more than half an hour now, Cobby," the old man observed. "It won't be long until they're upon us."

"What do they want with us?" Joel asked, raising his voice above the howling of the wind.

"They're buccaneers, Son," his father replied, moving his hand on the tiller to make a tiny correction in the cog's course. "Pirates."

"I know, Pa, but what would pirates want with us? The *Princess* is a fishing vessel. Surely they would know that we carry no gold or treasure."

"They want the *Princess* herself," Cobby replied. "A cog like this is worth a fair amount of money."

Joel swallowed hard. "If they take the *Princess*, what will they do with us?" In his fear, his voice trailed off so that the last few words were barely a whisper.

"Life is worth nothing to men like them," Wynn said gruffly, answering the question for his grandson. "If they seize the *Princess*, they'll kill us so that no word of their treachery gets out. Dead men tell no tales."

Joel trembled as he watched the pursuing ships. With a raucous screech, a seagull swooped down and perched momentarily on the spar of the mast and then almost instantly took flight again. Fear tightened in the youth's belly as he watched the bird. "Even the gulls know that we are doomed," he croaked.

The wind shrieked and howled. The *Princess* now seemed to tremble as she crested each wave.

"They'll never board us in these seas," Wynn told Cobby. Bracing his feet against the planking of the hull, he again lifted the spyglass and watched the pursuing caravels for a long moment. "Wait a minute! Unless my eyes deceive me, that's Blackheart on deck!"

"I wasn't going to say anything," Cobby shouted above the violence of the elements, "but I suspected as much. If that's Blackheart, rough seas won't stop him."

At these words, Joel felt a surge of panic. "Blackheart?" he echoed. "The scourge of the Seven Seas? The pirate who always tortures his victims?"

His father nodded.

Joel winced.

Bracing himself against the wind, Wynn studied the passing onshore landmarks and then made his way aft to speak with his son at the tiller. Joel joined the two men. "Son," Wynn said, "we're still half an hour from harbor; but at the rate they're gaining on us, the caravels will be alongside in mere minutes. What are your plans? There are two of them, and there is no way to outmaneuver them. And even if we surrender the *Princess*, you know what they will do."

Cobby let out his breath in a long sigh. "I only have one idea, and I don't really like it." He looked his father in the eye and shook his head in resignation. "I'm going to try to run the channel."

Wynn was aghast. "Between the Twin Sisters? Son, that's suicide! The *Princess* will be dashed to pieces on the rocks!"

Cobby shrugged. "It's our only chance. We can't outrun Blackheart and his caravels, but maybe we can still slip through his filthy hands. The *Princess* has a draft of nearly five feet, but if the seas are high enough, maybe we can make it through. But the caravels need nine or ten feet beneath their hulls, so they won't try to follow us through the channel. Pa, it's our only chance! And I'd rather lose my ship on the rocks than to have it fall into the hands of Blackheart and his crew of cutthroats."

Wynn shook his head. "We'll never make it, Cobby."

Cobby glanced at Joel. "Pa, what if Blackheart kills us both and then takes my son captive? I can't chance that."

His father was silent for a long moment. At last, he nodded. "Aye, Son, you made your point. Go for the channel."

The Twin Sisters were lonely, rocky islands lying less than two miles offshore from the harbor town of Seawell, the home port of the *Princess* and her proud owners. The channel of which Cobby spoke was a narrow, rocky passage of surging waters that divided one island from the other. No captain of any seagoing vessel, large or small, would ever attempt to enter the passage from the south as Cobby was intending.

Joel looked across the starboard gunwale and realized that the *Princess* was already sailing past the wooded shores of Elder Sister, the easternmost island of the Twin Sisters. He shuddered. Legend held that the island was home to a number of ferocious dragons, though he had never met anyone who could claim to have seen one. He took a deep breath and tried to shake off the overwhelming feelings of trepidation. Surely the legends were merely the inventions of drunken sailors—there were no such things as dragons.

He turned and studied the pursuing pirate ships and was dismayed to see that they were nearly within hailing distance and were closing fast. "Pa, will we make it to the channel? The pirates are almost upon us!"

"With Emmanuel's help, Son, we will."

"Will we make it through the channel? It's not wide enough or deep enough, is it?"

Keeping one hand on the tiller, the rugged fisherman threw his other arm around his son, pulled him close in an embrace, and then released him. "I'll give it my best, Son, I promise you that. The rest is up to Emmanuel."

Joel nodded, slightly reassured. He had the utmost confidence in his father's abilities as a sailor. A man of the sea since his childhood, Cobby had spent a lifetime on the waters, working aboard and eventually captaining fishing vessels like the cog. If it were humanly possible to sail the *Princess* through the channel, Cobby of Seawell was the man to do it.

"We'll reach the channel in about three minutes," Cobby told Wynn and Joel. "Get ready. Joel, get the oars out. I want you on the forward port oar. Pa, be ready to drop the sail the instant I call for it and then take the forward starboard oar. I'll stay at the tiller. Only with Emmanuel's help will we make it through this."

Joel glanced at the pursuing caravels. "Pa, they're less than fifty paces aft! They're closing fast!"

"Forget Blackheart and his crew," his father admonished. "Concentrate on one thing: rowing the *Princess* through the channel. We'll have the tide behind us, so basically we're just steering. And remember, we're in Emmanuel's mighty hands."

The wind shrieked and howled as the storm suddenly closed in. The skies were as black as an ink spill. Ten-foot swells tossed the struggling cog about erratically, shaking her violently one moment and dropping her into a deep trough the next. Lightning slashed down repeatedly from the darkened heavens to strike the seas about the *Princess* in dazzling displays of fiery power. Cold rain poured down in torrents. In the stern of the tossing vessel, Cobby wrestled with the tiller as he struggled to hold the cog to her course.

Thoroughly soaked and shaking with cold and fear, Joel stared through the maelstrom of shrieking wind and slashing rain, trying desperately to spot the pursuing pirate ships. But the violence of the tempest kept him from seeing anything. "Pa," he shouted, "maybe we can lose Blackheart in this storm! He can't follow us if he can't see us!"

At that moment, one of the pursuing caravels appeared out of the darkness of the tempest, less than ten yards off the *Princess'* port rail. A score of pirates lined the rail, laughing and jeering and waving cutlasses. "Give it up, friends!" one buccaneer shouted. "You'll never outrun us!" Raising his hand high, he hurled a dagger with such force that the blade buried itself in the mast of the *Princess*.

Joel fell to his knees, so overcome with terror that he could not even stand.

One pirate clung to a line hanging from a spar. As the surging waters thrust the two vessels toward each other, he gave a shrill cry and launched himself over the rail, swinging in a long arc toward the *Princess*. As he reached the end of his arc he seemed to realize that the distance was too great, so he simply swung back aboard the caravel and landed on the rail.

"Emmanuel, help us!" Joel cried aloud.

"Five feet closer and he would have had us," Wynn muttered.

The pirates cheered as their companion swung out again, but again the *Princess* was just out of range and so he swung back to the ship. The caravel abruptly disappeared into the storm as the tumultuous waters thrust the two vessels apart. A feeling of relief swept over Joel when the darkness of the tempest swallowed the pirate ship.

8

"Get ready!" Cobby shouted at Wynn. "Drop the sail when I give the order. We're getting close to the channel and we need to be ready to come about."

Clutching his oar, Joel stared hard into the crashing seas off the starboard beam. *How can Papa even tell where we are?* he wondered. *I can't see a thing through this storm!*

"Ready?" Cobby shouted.

"When you give the order, Son," Wynn shouted back.

At that instant the mast snapped with a sharp report like a crack of thunder. The shattered mast, sail, and rigging came tumbling down to cover the bow. Joel and Wynn leaped to one side to avoid the falling mast and rigging. The *Princess* rose high in the air on the crest of a gigantic wave, hesitated, and heeled over hard to starboard. "Oars in the water!" Cobby ordered. "Drag! Slow her down!"

Pulling his oar from beneath the debris, Joel thrust it deep into the surging waters and pulled hard against it. The long handle of the oar seemed to shudder as the currents fought against the blade.

Cobby leaned hard into the tiller and the *Princess* turned even more sharply to starboard and then seemed to leap forward as she entered the narrow channel between the two islands. From the bottom of the hull came a horrendous grinding, crunching sound and the entire ship shook. The bow spun sharply to port. "Starboard!" Cobby shouted. "Turn to starboard!" Joel dug in deeply with his oar, rowing frantically to help turn the vessel to starboard.

"Steady...steady," Cobby called. "Now, back to port a bit."

Working feverishly at the tiller and calling orders to his two oarsmen, the skilled fisherman guided the cog through the darkened channel. There were occasional bumps and scrapes as the wooden hull glided across submerged rocks, but the

THE ISLE OF DRAGONS

Princess was traversing the channel! Joel glanced up to realize that the passageway was somewhat protected from the violence of the storm; the wind had lessened dramatically and the rain no longer pounded them so relentlessly.

After they had struggled for several minutes to stay in the channel and keep the *Princess* from destruction on the rocks, the channel abruptly widened and the *Princess* sailed out into a secluded cove on the western end of Elder Sister. The storm ceased as abruptly as it had come, and a brilliant beam of golden sunlight played upon the waters. The *Princess* glided into the cove, drifted to a gentle stop in the very center, and then sat peacefully rocking to and fro.

Thirty yards from her bow stretched a pristine beach of the purest white sand, and just beyond that, sheer cliffs rose like the walls of a castle. On the south end of the cove, a sturdy dock gave way to a well-traveled trail that led toward the cliffs. To the north and the south of the cove, tall outcroppings of rugged ironshore protected the little bay from the force of the winds. It was though the island herself was holding the secluded cove in the protection of her ironshore arms.

"Praise be to Emmanuel!" Wynn exclaimed. "You did it, Son! The mast is destroyed, but we made it safely."

"We all did it," Cobby replied wearily. "And as you said, the praise belongs to King Emmanuel." He eyed the tangled debris covering the forward part of the cog. "The mast is beyond hope, but perhaps we can save the sail and the rigging."

Joel let out his breath in a long, noisy sigh. "We're still alive! I really didn't think we would make it! And the pirates can't get us here."

Wynn glanced around the cove, noting the beauty and serenity surrounding the *Princess*. "I never knew this inlet was here. It's a natural harbor." He frowned. "But what is that dock used for?"

"We're safe!" Joel exulted. "We escaped the pirates and we made it through the channel. We're safe!"

His father's face was grave as he walked forward to inspect the shattered mast and rigging. "Actually, we may be in greater danger than before," he replied quietly. "This is Elder Sister, better known as 'the Isle of Dragons.' Perhaps we would be safer facing the pirates than the dragons."

Chapter Two

Cobby, Wynn, and Joel sat quietly for several long minutes as they rested from their ordeal. Secured by bow and stern anchors, the *Princess* creaked contentedly as she rocked in the gentle swells that passed beneath her hull. "I'm sorry about the mast, Son," Wynn told Cobby. "I know that's a bit of a setback."

Cobby shrugged. "We didn't lose the *Princess*, and for that I am grateful. We're all safe, and for that I am especially grateful. The mast can be replaced."

"How long will it take to replace it?" Joel inquired.

"The three of us can cut a spruce pole in the forest tomorrow," his father replied. "We can take it to the shipyard and have Micah make a new mast while we repair the sail and the rigging. Once Micah and his crew set the mast, we'll install the rigging ourselves and then we'll be back in business. If all goes well, maybe a week."

"How are we going to get home?" Joel asked.

"We'll stay here for the night. If the storm is over in the morning, we'll row home. It will be quite a chore, but if we go with the tide, we can do it."

"Two miles," Wynn muttered. "I hate to think of rowing the *Princess* two miles."

Cobby laughed. "Pa, let's be thankful that we still have the *Princess*. I'm thankful we *can* row her home."

Wynn nodded. "I know, Son." He looked at the remains of the mast. "It will be dark soon, but why don't we work on salvaging the sail and the rigging? We can't row home with this mess hanging over the bow."

The three set to work clearing the twisted lines and rigging from the broken mast. It took just a moment or two to learn that although the mast and spar were both shattered beyond repair, the rigging and the sail were for the most part intact. "Looks like there's just one large tear in the sail," Wynn observed, with some satisfaction.

"That can easily be repaired," Cobby replied. "Joel, get on the end there—help me roll this sail up."

"I have to ask you something, Son," Wynn said, as he struggled with a knot in the rigging. "How did you know when to turn the boat into the channel? I was watching for the channel, but I couldn't see a thing through the storm. Visibility wasn't more than five or six yards at best. There is no way that you have seen the entrance to the channel, so how did you do it? How did you find it in such a storm?"

Cobby shrugged. "To be honest, I didn't. I knew we were close to the island and that we were approaching the channel, but I had no idea where it was."

His father frowned. "What do you mean, you didn't know? You turned the *Princess* at the precise moment and sailed her in perfectly. How did you know where the channel was?"

Cobby looked up from the crumpled sail. "If you remember, Pa, when the mast snapped, the cog turned hard to starboard. I didn't do it. A moment or two later I saw the channel entrance, but the *Princess* was already heading into it as if she knew exactly where to go."

Wynn shook his head. "That's—that's incredible!"

Joel was stunned. "Did Emmanuel do that? Did he break the mast so that our boat would turn into the channel?"

Cobby shrugged and nodded. "Aye, lad, so it appears. Perhaps he sent one or two of the shining ones to do it. At any rate, His Majesty was watching over us."

"That's amazing." Joel glanced up at the cliffs looming over the cove. "Hey—there are stairs up there!"

"Stairs? Where?" Wynn and Cobby turned as one to see the stairs to which Joel was referring.

"Look." Joel pointed. "There are stairs leading up into that crevice in the face of the cliff. Look, you can see a chain just above them that would serve as a handrail."

The men studied the face of the cliff. "There *are* stairs!" Wynn exclaimed. "Where in Terrestria do you suppose they lead to? And who would have built them?"

"Can we go ashore and explore them, Pa?" Joel asked. "I'd like to see where they go."

Cobby shook his head and a look of displeasure crossed his face. "Elder Sister is the Isle of Dragons, remember?" He raised his voice. "This island is inhabited by dragons and this is a place of danger. No, we are not going to explore the island and that's final."

"I just asked, Pa."

"Well, the answer is no and that's final."

Joel stared at him. *Why is he so upset that I asked to explore the island? It was just a simple question.* "Do you believe that there really are dragons here, Pa? I didn't think that dragons really existed."

"Aye, the dragons are very real and we are in very real danger just being here. That's the reason we are not going ashore. Now forget the stairs and help me finish with this sail, would you?"

"Aye, Pa." Joel cast one final glance at the mysterious stairs and then bent to the task of salvaging the sail and rigging.

The stars were brilliant. The *Princess* rocked gently in the swells and the water lapped persistently at the hull. Joel lay with his face to the sky, using the seine net for a mattress. One corner of the sail was pulled over him for the little bit of warmth that it afforded. Papa Wynn was sound asleep beside him.

Joel let out a sigh as he thought about the events of that evening. The broken mast and spar had been tossed overboard; the rigging had been neatly coiled in the bow; and the sail had been carefully rolled up and stashed along the port rail. The three fishermen had worked feverishly, and the project had been finished before complete darkness had descended. Supper had been scanty: pieces of hardtack washed down with water.

Joel tossed and turned. Exhausted as he was, he was mildly surprised that sleep was eluding him.

He turned and glanced toward the bow where Pa stood watch with a large net hook in his hands. *He holds it like a weapon,* Joel told himself. *What is he watching for? What is he afraid of? The cove seems to be a place of peace and safety, yet he's been uneasy ever since we got here. Are there really dragons here?*

He looked beyond the bow to the towering cliffs which now gleamed silver-white in the moonlight. *I wonder where the stairs lead. Pa says that the island is inhabited by dragons, but there must be people here, too, for the dragons would not have built the stairs.* He sighed wistfully. *I still would like to follow those stairs and see where they go. I'd love to explore this entire island!*

Just then the moon slipped behind a cloud, plunging the cove and the cliffs into darkness. Joel glanced toward the top of the cliffs and then inhaled sharply. The summit of the cliff was defined by a line of softly glowing blue-white lights! As he watched in fascination, the line of lights slowly moved along the edge of the precipice and then one by one winked out as they reached the far corner. Moments later they began to re-appear one by one halfway down the cliff and then float down toward the cove at an angle. Mystified, Joel trembled as he watched, afraid to move, almost afraid to breathe. *How could the lights simply float down the face of the cliff?*

Suddenly it dawned on him—the lights were following the stairs that he had seen earlier that evening. *So I was right. The stairs do go all the way to the top of the cliffs.* As he continued to watch, the blue lights descended all the way to the base of the cliff and then slowly made their way along the beach.

Joel's heart began to pound. *Who or what is carrying the lights? What if they're coming here? What if they attack the boat?* He glanced at Pa, but Pa hadn't even noticed the long line of lights. *How could he not see them?* Joel wondered.

The mysterious lights continued across in front of the cliff and then winked out one by one as if they had dropped into a hole. Puzzled, Joel could not even venture a guess as to what was taking place.

Moments later, as the endless line of lights continued to disappear one by one, other lights began to reappear and make their way back across the beach and up the face of the cliff. Before long, two solid lines of soft blue-white lights were traveling in both directions. *It's like watching an army of ants,* Joel thought sleepily. *Hundreds of little ants, all carrying little blue lights...*

Moments later, he was sound asleep.

Strong hands seized his shoulder and shook him violently. Terrified, Joel opened his eyes to find that he was staring up into the stern face of his father. Relief flooded over him. "Joel, wake up," Cobby said again. "We need to get moving so that we can catch the tide when it starts in."

Joel sat up and rubbed his eyes. "Pa, did you see anything last night?"

"See anything? Such as...?"

"Oh, anything unusual. Strange lights or anything like that?"

"Strange lights? Son, what are you talking about?"

"I just wondered if you saw—oh, never mind."

Papa Wynn laughed and Joel looked over at him. "He was dreaming, Cobby. Last night was a rough night and he was dreaming."

"Aye, well, let's dream that we're rowing the *Princess* across to Seawell Harbor, shall we? The channel leading out is much wider and safer than the one we took in, but we have to hurry if we're going to take advantage of that incoming tide." He glanced uneasily across the cove. "Even in broad daylight this place gives me the shivers."

The morning sun sparkled on the waters of Seawell Harbor as the *Princess* glided past a small fleet of five or six fishing boats that were preparing to put out to sea. The entire fleet was owned by Theros, one of the wealthiest men in Seawell. "Home at last," Wynn sang out. "That was a fair bit of work to get here."

"Quit your grumbling, Pa," Cobby replied good-naturedly. "We both have to admit that the *Princess* brought us across faster than we had anticipated."

"Just over an hour by my reckoning," Joel piped up.

"I think you're about right, Son. The incoming tide did most of the work for us, but it sounds like your grandfather wants most of the credit." Wynn and Joel both laughed at this remark.

"Ahoy, Wynn and Cobby!" one boat captain called out as the cog approached. "You forgot your mast!" His laughter rang out across the water.

The other sailors all paused in their work to stare at the damaged vessel. Many of them laughed at the strange sight of a fishing cog without a mast, but others were sympathetic. "What happened, Cobby?" one fisherman called as Wynn and Joel rowed past his vessel. "Did you get caught in the storm last night?"

Cobby nodded. "Aye. It was a rough one. Did anyone else sustain any damage to their boats?"

"Nay, not really," came the reply. "We got a bit of a blow last night, but nothing that would do much damage. I think we missed the worst of the storm. Where did you lay by last night?"

Cobby gestured over his shoulder with his thumb. "We spent the night in the cove between the Twin Sisters."

The other man gave a low whistle. "You're a braver man than I, Cobby. I think I'd rather spend the night on the open sea than go anywhere near the Twin Sisters." He glanced at the stump of the broken mast and shook his head sympathetically. "I hope the mast replacement goes smoothly."

"I thank you," Cobby replied, as the *Princess* moved out of earshot.

Moments later as the vessel glided into her usual berth at the dock, Joel dropped his oar and sprang forward. Seizing the bow line, he wrapped it around a stanchion and tied the vessel securely. Cobby had the stern line secured before he had finished.

"Pa, would you run over to the shipyard and ask for Micah?" Cobby requested. "Tell him what happened and that we'll bring the *Princess* and a spruce pole to him before this evening. Ask him how much time he'll need and what he'll charge to shape and set the mast and make the spar. Tell him that we'll varnish it ourselves and that we'll install the rigging ourselves."

Wynn nodded. "Aye, Son."

"Joel, run home and get the cart from the shed. We might as well take the nets home and work on them while the boat is down. Poke your head in the door and tell your ma that we're all right, but don't say anything about the pirates. Tell her that I hoped she wouldn't lose any sleep last night and that we should be home within the hour."

Flat-footed, Joel leaped the railing and landed on the dock. "Right away, Pa."

Cobby laughed. "You make me feel old every time you do that."

"I do it so that I won't get old," Joel replied with a grin, and then darted away. Moments later, as he strode briskly up the steep lane leading to the humble cottage that he shared with his parents and grandfather, he paused and looked out over the harbor. From this vantage the *Princess* looked like a toy boat. He could see Papa Wynn making his way along the pier toward the shipyards while Cobby worked at separating the fishing nets in the *Princess*.

"Hey, Red!" a taunting voice called. "Whacha looking at?"

Joel turned as three youth came sauntering down the lane toward him. His stomach tightened when he saw them. The tallest of the three, a young man named Lank, was the insolent son of Theros, the wealthiest of Seawell's fishing fleet owners. Usually referred to as a "do-nothing" by the towns-people because of his lack of initiative or direction, Lank was known throughout Seawell as a trouble-maker. More than once his wealthy father had been forced to pay for damages that Lank and his gang of toughs had inflicted upon some property owner. Tall and good-looking, the troublesome youth was a natural leader, and, in spite of his bad reputation, was openly admired by many of the young men and sought after by many of the young ladies of Seawell.

"Whacha looking at, Red?" Lank asked again as he approached. "Something sure has your attention."

"The name is not Red," Joel retorted, doing his best to maintain his composure in spite of the taunting. The one thing that Joel could not stand was teasing about his flaming red hair. "Lay off, Lank."

"If your hair was blond I'd call you Yellow," Lank replied, and his two companions laughed at the foolish remark. "What should I call you, Red?"

"You know my name."

Lank reached for Joel's temple and Joel batted his hand away. "Hey, don't be so touchy," Lank said, pooching out his lower lip to mock him. "I just wanna touch your hair—wanna see if it's as hot as it looks."

Joel turned away.

"Hey, Red," Lank taunted, gazing down at the harbor, "your pa walks like a duck. Look at him! He walks just like a duck."

Joel glanced down at the *Princess* and saw his father walking along the dock with his usual limp. "Leave my pa alone," Joel replied through clenched teeth. "He limps because of a leg injury. Pa was wounded in battle long before you were even born. His limp is a badge of honor."

"Oh, really?" Lank sneered. He bent his knees and walked

toward Joel, flapping his hands at his sides. "Look at me—I'm a duck, but I was wounded in battle. It's a badge of honor." His companions hooted with laughter.

Encouraged by their reactions, Lank continued with the silly charade and paraded back and forth with bent knees. "Cobby Cobby Cobby Cobby."

"Lank, I thought you said you were a duck," Marcus said, doubled over with laughter, "but you sound more like a turkey!" Imitating Lank, the boy bent his knees and called, "Cobby Cobby Cobby. Gobble gobble gobble."

"Look, guys, that's enough!" Joel stormed. "Pa is more of a man than any of you will ever be. Leave him alone."

"What are you going to do about it, Red?" the third boy, Dade, challenged.

Joel shrugged, trying not to look as nervous as he felt. "I can flatten any one of you," he replied fiercely, though inside he felt anything but fierce. "I'll fight any one of you, but I'm not gonna take on all three."

Marcus stepped forward and grabbed Joel's tunic, but Lank swatted him on the shoulder and then brushed him aside. "Hey, fellows, take a walk. Joel and I need to talk. I'll catch up with you in a couple of minutes."

Without a word of argument, both of Lank's companions shrugged and sauntered down the lane toward the harbor. "As you wish, Lank."

As Lank turned to Joel, the younger boy felt his stomach tighten. What did Lank want now? He wasn't prepared for Lank's words. "Hey, look, Joel—I'm sorry."

Joel stared at Lank. "Would you say that again?"

"Aye, Joel. I'm sorry. Hey, look—I didn't know you were so sensitive about your hair, all right? I'll leave you alone. Can we be friends?"

Joel hesitated, taken aback by the abruptness of Lank's apology.

"Hey, the guys think it's funny but I'll tell them to leave you alone, too. Can we be friends?"

Joel studied Lank's face, trying to determine the sincerity of his words.

"Look, Joel," Lank said quietly, stepping closer and putting a hand on Joel's shoulder like an old friend, "the only reason I pick on you and your father is because I'm jealous of you."

Joel turned to face him. "Jealous? Of me? Why?"

Lank shrugged. "I guess I'm just jealous of you because of your pa. The two of you always work together so closely, but my pa doesn't even know that I exist. He's always so busy running all his 'business enterprises' as he calls them that he never has any time for me. I'd give anything to have a Pa like yours."

Joel was silent as he thought it through.

"So anyway," Lank continued, "if you can forgive me, I'd like to have you as a friend. Can you do that?"

Joel nodded. "Sure, Lank, sure. I'd like to count you as my friend."

"Great!" Lank responded. "Thanks, pal. Hey—I gotta run, catch up with the others. I'll see you around."

"Aye, Lank, I'll see you around." As Joel turned toward home, he wondered what had caused the incredible change in Lank's attitude toward him.

Had he seen Lank's sneering grin, he would have realized that he was walking into a trap.

Chapter Three

The *Princess* bounded eagerly through the surging waves as if delighted to be on the high seas again as the three fishermen took her for a trial run. Joel was at the tiller. He held a course that paralleled the shoreline, sailing along an imaginary line that ran midway between Seawell and the Twin Sisters. Behind the boat, glass floats bobbed in the surf, indicating the presence of the large seine net towed by the *Princess*. A flock of gulls passed overhead, squawking and scolding each other as they flew over.

Wynn stood at the base of the mast, looking upward as if fascinated by the billowing sail. "The mast and spar are perfect, Son!" he called to Cobby, who stood in the bow surveying the blue-gray waters.

"Micah has never let us down," Cobby replied. "What did you expect?"

"Why so quiet today?"

Cobby shrugged. "I was hoping to pull in at least a small catch this afternoon while we did the trial run. But we haven't caught a thing."

Wynn snorted. "You know better than to fish this close to town."

Cobby shrugged. "I didn't want to sail that far from home until we had a chance to test the new mast."

Joel looked up as a brown pelican flew over with a fish sticking out of its oversized bill. "At least the pelicans are fishing well."

"That's enough out of you," Cobby snapped, and then turned toward the stern with a wide grin to let Joel know that he was jesting.

Joel spotted a flurry of activity off the port bow a league or two away and glanced in that direction to see a flock of seagulls fluttering and swooping just above the surface of the water. At this distance he could not hear their raucous cries, but he knew exactly what they were doing. "Pa, look!" he said, pointing. "Shall I follow the gulls?"

"By all means," Cobby replied, striding toward the stern. "I'll take the tiller now."

"Let him keep it," Wynn said.

Cobby stared at his father. "What?"

"Let Joel stay at the tiller."

"There's a school of cod or hake just waiting for us to come along and swoop them up," Cobby argued. "Do you think I want to miss that?"

"The *Princess* won't get there one second sooner with you at the helm," Wynn told him. "Let the boy stay where he is. He's doing fine."

Cobby opened his mouth to protest but Wynn held up one hand. "Listen to me, Son. You wouldn't be the outstanding fisherman that you are today if I hadn't let you take the tiller when you were his age."

Cobby grinned. "Maybe I never said it before, but thanks, Pa." Wynn grinned back and thumped him on the shoulder.

As the cog approached the school of fish, Pa let out a low whistle. "This is a big one, boys. Joel, hold your course until the *Princess* passes the entire school and then turn hard to port. After another fifty yards or so, turn back to starboard."

Wynn said, "Cobby."

Cobby looked at him.

"This is Joel's catch, remember? He knows what he's doing."

Cobby nodded and held up both hands as if in surrender. "Aye. Sorry."

Wynn laughed.

Moments later the *Princess* slowed abruptly. "What happened, Pa?" Joel cried out.

Cobby looked astern. "Nothing, Son—you just filled the nets with several tons of cod and hake; that's all." He grinned broadly. "Head for the harbor, Son, and tell the *Princess* to give you all she's got! This may be the biggest catch in her history!"

The *Princess* responded sluggishly to the tiller as Joel turned her hard to starboard and headed back toward the harbor. Behind the stern, the huge seine net teemed with fish—a record catch. "If you wanted to test the new mast, Son, you're doing it," Wynn told Cobby with a delighted chuckle. "The *Princess* has never taken such a strain as she has now. If she can handle this large a catch, she can handle anything."

Cobby laughed. "Wouldn't I like to be at the helm as we enter the harbor with a catch like this," he complained, but his eyes twinkled, and Wynn knew that he was proud of his son. "I should get at least part of the credit."

The Seawell harbor buzzed with activity as the *Princess* sailed proudly in with her record catch. Most of the fleets had just gotten in and were tending to their catches and equipment when the cog came gliding by, struggling against the fully loaded nets. "Would you look at that!" one fisherman exclaimed when he saw the *Princess*. Leaping from his own boat up to the dock, he ran alongside Cobby's vessel. "Where were you fishing today, Cobby?"

"Just a mile from here," Cobby replied grandly. "We were halfway between the harbor and the Twin Sisters."

Joel looked up to realize that a number of fishermen were running along the dock in an effort to see their catch. "Take her all the way to the fishmonger," Cobby instructed. "With a catch of this size, I doubt if he'll mind us using his dock to unload."

❧

"Just over four hundred fifty-one stone," the fishmonger told Cobby. "That's more than three tons of fish! You brought them in at just the right time, too. Right now we're paying top prices." Cobby, Wynn, and Joel watched in fascinated silence as the man counted a large number of gold and silver coins into a cloth sack. "Come back when you have a catch worth weighing," he said with a teasing grin. "These piddly little catches are hardly worth my time."

He handed the money to Cobby. "I'm glad you did so well, my friend."

"Won't Ma be delighted when she hears about this catch," Cobby remarked as they slowly rowed the *Princess* back to her berth. "This is by far the largest one we have ever had in one day."

"Six hundred and twelve klorins," Wynn said thoughtfully. "Cobby, if we use our emergency savings, we have slightly more than enough to pay off the note on the *Princess*!"

Cobby stared at him. "Pa, you're right. And this is the last day of the month, right?"

Wynn nodded.

"If we can get it to the moneylenders tonight, we'll save a month's usury."

Wynn glanced at the sky. "They're five miles from here and they close shop in about an hour. We'd never make it home and back to Darwick in time. Who's going to tend to the nets and the boat if we do try to take it tonight?"

"Pa, I can take it on foot!" Joel said eagerly. "If I leave now I can make it in time."

"This is a lot of money, Son," Cobby said soberly. "If anything should happen to it...."

"Pa, I'll run the whole way. I've been to the moneylenders with you before, so I know the way. Please, Pa."

Cobby hesitated.

"In a way, it is his catch," Wynn remarked. "Let him take it, Cobby. We can tend to the *Princess* and the nets while he's gone."

Cobby stepped to the stern, pulled a large leather wallet from the small hold, and slid the sack of coins into it. "Have them count it in front of you, then," he instructed, "and make sure that they give you a receipt before you leave the premises. As a matter of fact, since you're paying off the loan, they should sign off on the lien note and give it to you."

Wynn gave him a delighted grin. "As of tonight, the *Princess* is ours, free and clear!"

Cobby's smile was just as exuberant. "Praise Emmanuel. Out of debt after all these years! That's a good feeling."

"We had better pull close to the dock and let the lad be on his way," Wynn reminded. "Time is wasting, you know."

"Go by the stables and ask Thane for a fast horse," Cobby suggested. "Tell him that one of us will stop in tomorrow and pay him whatever he wants to charge. That will save you some walking and make sure that you get the payment there in time.

Stop by the house and ask your ma for the emergency savings. She'll know what you mean."

Fifteen minutes later, Joel sat astride a tall, gray mare with a fast gait. As he left the city limits he urged the mare to a gallop. The heavy wallet bounced against his side as he rode. Just as the mare entered the shadows of a copse of cedars, a rabbit leaped from the grasses and bounded across the road, passing between the mare's feet. Spooked, the horse reared high, throwing her young rider from the saddle to strike his head against a rocky ledge. Everything went black.

When he awoke, Joel found that he was lying in tall grasses at the side of a well-traveled road. The sun had set and night was almost upon him. *Where am I?* he wondered as he sat up. *How did I get here?* Shakily, he stood to his feet, looking around in bewilderment. *What am I doing out here?*

The *moneylenders! I was going to the moneylenders in Darwick.* His mind cleared just a bit, and, remembering his errand, he started in the proper direction. He had gone just a few steps when he realized that something didn't feel right. *A horse! I was riding a horse!* He looked around. *But where is it?*

His head ached and he felt quite dizzy. Bracing himself against a tree, he took a deep breath and struggled to make sense of the situation. *I was going to the moneylenders,* he told himself, *and I was riding a horse. I remember that much. But where is the horse and why was I going to the moneylenders?*

He started down the road, walking slowly and carefully as he tried to recall his errand. *I was going to the moneylenders to... to pay off the loan on the Princess!* The thought cheered him. *Pa and Papa Wynn gave me money to pay off the lien on the boat—that's why I'm going to the moneylenders.* He patted his side and then a dreadful feeling swept over him. *The wallet! Where is it?*

Joel stood still in the middle of the roadway, confused and disoriented. *Where is the wallet?*

Slowly, painstakingly, he retraced his steps as he searched for the missing wallet in the dying light. His thinking cleared slowly, and by the time he reached the place where the mare had thrown him he was lucid enough to recognize the spot. He found the crumpled grass where he had lain beside the roadway, and then the mare's tracks, and...wait, what was this?

The mare's tracks were plainly visible in the dust at the edge of the roadway. Even in the subdued light, Joel could see at least two pairs of human tracks leading away from the spot where he had fallen. In places, the human tracks obscured the mare's tracks. He inhaled sharply as he realized what that meant. At least two people had come along after the mare had thrown him—when he was unconscious! His heart sank. *So that's where the wallet went.*

Disheartened by the discovery, he turned and began to trudge back toward town. He had hardly gone two hundred paces when he heard a horse whinny and saw a dark silhouette beneath a sweet gum tree. His heart pounded as he hurried over to the horse. He let out a sigh when he saw that the saddle was empty. "Finding you and the wallet would be too much to hope for," he told the horse as he swung gingerly into the saddle. "What is Pa going to say when I tell him that I lost all that money?"

Joel had ridden three or four furlongs when he spotted a flickering amber glow deep in the forest to his right. Curious, he dismounted and carefully tied the mare to a tree. Moving slowly and silently, he slipped from tree to tree, making no more noise than a Nidian scout. When he reached the source of the amber light his breath caught in his throat.

In the center of a small clearing a small fire crackled and popped, occasionally sending glowing sparks skyward. Kneeling on the ground beside the fire were Lank and two other young men with a wallet on the ground between them. Pa's wallet! Right beside the wallet was a pile of gold and silver coins which the young men were busily counting into three smaller piles. Lank and his companions were dividing the money intended to pay off the lien on the *Princess*!

Joel stepped into the circle of firelight. "Lank, am I glad to see you!"

His sudden appearance startled the three youths. As they leaped to their feet, the eldest uttered an oath and grabbed Joel by the collar, drawing a dagger in the same motion. "Who are you?" The dagger pressed hard against Joel's throat.

"Th-that's my pa's w-wallet," Joel managed to stammer. "I—I lost it when my horse threw me."

The dagger never wavered. "Liar! This money is ours from a job we did. We just got paid today."

"The wallet is my pa's," Joel replied evenly. He looked at Lank. "Tell him, Lank. Tell him that the money is ours."

Lank wouldn't meet his gaze. "How do I know it's yours?"

"The wallet is Pa's," Joel protested. "I'd know it anywhere."

The dagger was removed from Joel's throat. "Give him the wallet and get him out of here," the owner said. "We don't need the wallet."

"The money is Pa's, too," Joel insisted. "I was taking it to the moneylenders when my horse threw me." He paused as a sudden thought occurred. "You took the wallet from me!" he accused Lank. "I was unconscious and you took it from me!"

Lank said nothing but looked very uncomfortable.

"The money is ours," the owner of the dagger told him.

"Here." He reached down and retrieved the wallet, handing it to Joel. "You can keep the wallet."

"I'm not leaving without the money," Joel insisted. "It's ours and you know it."

"I'm about to lose patience with you, knave. You had better get out of here before I decide to slit your throat." Joel looked into the cruel eyes of the speaker and knew that it was not an empty threat. Without a word he took the wallet and hurried through the trees, glancing back from time to time to be certain that he was not being followed.

Joel was untying the horse when he heard voices. Stepping behind a thicket, he waited.

"He had to have come this way," a familiar voice said.

"Perhaps the moneylenders can tell us what happened," replied a second familiar voice, "if we can find them at this hour."

Relief flooded over Joel as he stepped into the roadway. "Pa! Papa Wynn!"

Wynn and Cobby were so startled that they both cried out and grabbed each other.

"Pa, am I glad to see you!"

"Joel! Joel, what are you doing here? What happened?"

Breathlessly, Joel told the story.

Cobby frowned when he had finished. "So where is the money? Where are these ruffians?"

Joel pointed toward the amber glow. "We're not more than a hundred yards from them."

Wynn looked at Cobby. "What are you going to do, Son?"

"There's only one thing to do, Pa." Cobby searched the underbrush until he located a stout limb to use as a quarterstaff. "I'm gonna thrash me some skunks and get our money back."

Cobby squared his shoulders. "You know how to move

quietly," he told Joel and Wynn. "Let's do it. Joel, lead the way."

Joel's heart pounded as he, his father, and his grandfather slipped through the woods as noiselessly as three phantoms. At the edge of the clearing he paused and his father slipped up beside him. Joel pointed. The money was now in three separate piles. Lank and his companions were arguing as to the share that each would get. "I say we split it three ways even," Lank was saying.

"Who saw the kid first?" the owner of the dagger argued. "Who found the money? I did. I still say that one-fourth belongs to me for that very reason; then we divide the other three-fourths evenly."

"Aye, Justin, as if we couldn't have found it without your help," the third youth replied scornfully. "The kid was lying there as big as you please. Do you really think we were going to just walk right by without seeing him?"

"Don't mock me, Abez, or you'll wish you hadn't," Justin threatened.

"We split it three ways," Lank insisted again. "There's plenty for each of us."

Cobby stepped into the firelight. "Allow me to save you some time, lads," he said in a loud voice, startling the three ruffians. "The money is ours, as my son has already told you."

Justin leaped between Cobby and the money, drawing the dagger as he did. "The money is ours, old man, so don't get any ideas about taking it. We found it fair and it's ours now."

"You took it from my son after he had his accident," Cobby replied evenly. He took a step forward. "Don't talk of 'finding' it. You stole it, lads, stole it from an unconscious traveler."

Justin stalked forward with the dagger held menacingly. "Try touching it, old man, and you're dead."

"The money is ours and I intend to return home with it," Cobby told him.

Joel's heart pounded furiously.

With a snarl of rage, Justin leaped forward, slashing fiercely at Cobby with the dagger. The fisherman simply side-stepped, and as the ruffian lunged past him, rapped him across the shoulders with the quarterstaff, knocking him face down in the dirt. Justin leaped to his feet, whirled around, and lunged at Cobby again. Cobby calmly stooped and swung the stave, knocking Justin's feet from under him and sending him tumbling. When the furious youth came at him a third time, the fisherman repeated the maneuver and again sent him tumbling.

It was then that Joel realized that his father was in no real danger. Rather than simply knocking him to the ground and disarming him, Cobby was toying with Justin, deliberately drawing the conflict out to humiliate him in front of his friends. Awed, he looked at his father in a whole new light.

"I'll kill you, old man!" Justin screamed. "No one does this to me and gets away with it! I'll kill you!"

To Joel's astonishment, his father calmly tossed the quarterstaff to one side and beckoned with both hands. "When you're ready, lad."

With a snarl of rage, Justin raised the dagger and leaped upon the fisherman, who calmly side-stepped at the last instant. Grasping Justin's right wrist with one hand and his elbow with the other, Cobby flipped his assailant head over heels, twisting his arm behind him and pinning him to the ground. "I don't want to hurt you, lad, but if you don't release this dagger, I will break your arm."

Justin cursed and struggled.

Cobby increased the pressure. "This is the last time I'll say this," he growled. "Release the dagger or I will break your arm."

Justin released the dagger.

"Now listen to me and listen closely," Cobby told the cowed young man in a voice that was almost a growl, "when I release you, you and your friends are going to walk out of here as fast as you can go. If you do not, you will always wish that you had. Do you understand me?"

Justin nodded.

"I didn't hear you."

"Aye, sir," Justin whimpered.

Cobby maintained the pressure on Justin's arm. "Lank, you and Abez head for the road, now. Justin will be right behind you."

"Aye, sir." Lank and Abez seemed only too happy to leave. Without a backward glance they fled the clearing.

"Joel, gather up our money and return it to the wallet."

Joel obeyed and then said, "I have it all, Pa." He slung the strap of the wallet over his shoulder.

It was only then that Cobby let Justin up. The young man was actually trembling as he stood to his feet. Cobby rammed the blade of the dagger into the trunk of a tree and then twisted it, snapping the blade. He then tossed the handle to Justin, who caught it with shaky hands. "I hope that one day you'll start choosing to do what is right, lad, before you hurt yourself or someone else. Now, get out of here."

Justin fled.

Joel stared at his father, amazed at the fight that had just taken place. "That—that was incredible, Pa! Where did you learn to fight like that?"

Cobby shrugged and side-stepped the question as easily as he had side-stepped his assailant's attacks. "Let's go home."

As the three generations of fishermen left the woods, the youngest shook his head in amazement, astounded by what he had just witnessed. He had always respected his father as a man of integrity, unusual common sense, and great wisdom, a man who seemed to know what to do in almost any situation. He had always enjoyed being in Cobby's presence, for his father was consistently kind and gentle with him. But tonight he had seen a whole new side to Cobby of Seawell—apparently, the quiet fisherman was fearless, unafraid of anyone or anything.

There would come a time when that very quality would save Joel's life.

Chapter Four

"You should have seen Pa!" Joel told his mother as she served the evening meal. "He went against Justin bare-handed, even though Justin had a dagger. It was incredible! When Justin attacked with the dagger, Pa took it away from him. You would have been impressed!"

Ruth nodded. "Aye, I always have been." She placed a steaming dish of boiled potatoes on the table and turned back to the hearth.

"I doubt that Justin will ever tussle with us again," Joel exulted. "Right, Pa?"

"Who is this Justin?" Ruth asked.

"Just another do-nothing that I've seen around Seawell the last few months," Cobby replied. "I usually see him in the company of Lank."

"He's a bit older than Lank, though," Papa Wynn remarked, reaching for a mug and a pitcher of water. "I'd say he's three or four years older."

Ruth shook her head to show her disgust. "Perchance that's where that Lank gets some of his foolish notions. That boy is good for nothing."

"Lank is hardly a boy, Ma. He's nineteen years old."

"Aye, well, he acts like a child. You hear me, Joel; keep your distance from those ruffians! They're up to no good. Remember, 'a companion of fools shall be destroyed.' The King's own book warns youth about the company they keep."

Cobby smiled. "I think Joel is wiser than to keep company with the likes of them." He winked at Joel. "Tell your ma the good news—tell her about your catch today."

"Ma," Joel said, as his mother sat down at the table, "we had a record catch today! Guess what the total weight was."

Ruth shook her head. "I have no idea."

"Guess, Ma. Guess big."

"Two hundred stone."

"Higher."

"Three hundred stone."

"Higher."

Ruth stared at Cobby. "You caught more than three hundred stone of fish?"

Cobby grinned at her. "More than twice that, my love."

"Twice that..." Ruth's eyes grew wide. "So how much was this big catch worth in klorins, Sir Successful Fisherman?"

"Let's just say that the *Princess* now belongs to Pa and me, debt free! We'll be going to the moneylenders tomorrow to pay off the loan. That's where Joel was going when Lank and his cronies robbed him."

Ruth gave a cry of delight. "Pay off the *Princess*? Oh, Cobby, that's wonderful!" She leaned over and kissed him.

"Actually," Cobby told her, "the credit goes to Joel. He was at the tiller when we netted a whole school of cod with some hake mixed in with them."

"He also was the one who spotted the gulls and knew there was a school of fish there," Papa Wynn said proudly.

Ruth smiled at Joel. "You're going to be an outstanding

fisherman, Son, just like your father and grandfather."

❧

The loan on the *Princess* was paid off the very next day. Taking the morning off from fishing, Cobby, Joel, and Papa Wynn sailed the five miles to the town of Darwick to make sure that the money arrived safely. The moneylenders, after hearing Joel's story, agreed to waive the next month's interest even though the loan was already half a day into the next month. "We're debt-free," Cobby exulted, as they sailed back to Seawell. "The *Princess* is finally ours! It's a dream come true."

"She's a fine ship, Cobby," Papa Wynn replied. "You'll get many more years of service from her, I'm sure."

As the *Princess* bumped against the dock, Cobby turned to Joel. "Run over to the glassblowers and see if they have made our new floats yet. The net rides awfully low in the water and we need to replace the broken floats as soon as possible."

"I went yesterday morning, Pa. They told me to come back after the first of next week."

"So go again today."

"Pa, they won't have the floats ready. There's no sense in having me walk all the way over there for nothing."

"Go anyway."

"They're just going to get mad at me! If I show up again to-day asking about the floats, they're going to tell me to—"

"Son, not another word!" Cobby interrupted. "Quit arguing with me and go. Now."

"Aye, Pa." Angry at his father's insistence that he make a useless trip to the glassblowers' shop, Joel turned on his heel and strode quickly away. *This is all for nothing*, he told himself. *What's the point of checking when we know the floats won't be ready for several more days?*

Moments later, as he entered the glass shop, the proprietor looked up from his work. "May I help you, Joel?"

"I just came to check on the floats for Pa's nets."

The glassblower frowned. "Don't you ever listen? What did I tell you yesterday?"

"You said they wouldn't be ready till next week."

Irritation showed in the man's face. "See?" He threw up both hands and gave Joel a look of disgust. "If you heard me say that the floats won't be ready for several more days, why in Terrestria are you here bothering me about them again?" He leaned close and raised his voice until he was almost shouting. "The floats will be ready after the first of the week, all right? Please, lad, use your head! Don't come around here pestering me every day about the floats when I've already told you that they aren't ready!"

He shook his head, and the look on his face showed that he was disgusted with Joel. "Now run along—I have work to do. And please don't come back until after the first of the week."

Another customer had entered the shop just moments earlier, and, having heard part of the exchange, gave Joel a look of derision as he approached the workbench.

Joel's face was burning as he turned away. *Don't yell at me, you old goat!* he thought angrily. *I'm not the one who decided that I needed to check on those worthless floats! If you want to yell at somebody, yell at Pa!* Embarrassed and humiliated, he stormed from the shop. *This is all Pa's fault! I tried to tell him that the floats weren't ready, but does he listen to me? Nay. I have to walk all the way over here even though I know that it's pointless. And I'm the one who gets yelled at!*

Seething with anger, he strode down the street. *I'm the one who spotted the schools of cod and hake and netted a record catch! We paid off the Princess because of me. Pa and Papa Wynn now own her outright. And what do I get? Not one word of thanks, that's what!*

"Hey, what's the hurry?" A heavy hand on his shoulder slowed him down and he turned, irritated at the delay. He was surprised to find himself looking into the face of Lank. The ruffian was accompanied by two young men and a girl. "Where are you going in such a hurry?" Lank asked.

Joel pulled away. "Get away from me, Lank. You're no friend of mine."

Lank stepped back and help up both hands. "Wait, Joel. I just came to apologize."

"I really don't want to hear it, Lank."

"Please hear me. I beg you." A pitiful look crossed his face and Joel hesitated. "The money last night—I didn't know it was yours. Honest. Justin and Abez told me that they had found it."

"Don't tell me that," Joel growled. "You took it from me when I was unconscious."

"I—I wasn't there when it happened," Lank lied. "They told me that they found it."

"They were going to split it with you," Joel argued.

"Aye, we split a lot of things," Lank replied. "We're friends. But after what happened last night, I'm thinking of ending the friendship."

"Why should I believe that?"

"You don't see me with them today, do you?"

Joel glanced at Lank's companions, who nodded reassuringly. He paused to consider Lank's statement.

"I never would have intended to keep the money if I had known that it was yours," Lank told him suavely. "When you told Justin it was your pa's, I thought you were trying to steal it from us. I had no idea that you were telling the truth."

Joel hesitated.

"I'll tell you what I'll do to show you that my heart is in the right place," Lank offered. "I want to invite you to go to the Dragon Tournament with me. Tonight."

Joel stared at him. "Dragon Tournament? What in Terrestria...?"

"A Dragon Tournament is the most thrilling, most exciting event you've ever seen in your life," Lank told him, and his eyes seemed to light up as he said it. "If you've never been to a Dragon Tournament, you don't know what you're missing!"

Joel's pulse quickened and his heart pounded with excitement. Although he wasn't quite sure what a Dragon Tournament was, the very name suggested thrills and adventure. Once or twice he had heard whispered rumors about the Tournament, but it wasn't talked about openly and he had the idea that it was just for the elite. He did know that to be invited was a great honor. "Why are you inviting me?"

Lank laughed. "Oh, I just thought that you would enjoy it."

"When is it?"

"Tonight. Can you meet me at the docks three hours after sunset?"

Joel snorted. "My father would never let me do that, Lank."

Lank laughed derisively. "So who's going to ask your father?" Lank's companions laughed at this, and Joel glanced at them.

"Let me think about it."

"Come on, Joel, we need to know now. And believe me, no one is going to tell your father. He'll never know."

Ordinarily, Joel would never have considered such a proposition. The idea of doing anything behind his father's back would have been rejected immediately, for the young fisherman deeply respected his father and never questioned his father's deep love for him. Joel glanced at Lank's companions and saw that all three were grinning at him. Were they mocking him? Joel wasn't sure.

The girl spoke up. "Are you afraid?"

Joel laughed as if to prove himself. "Afraid? Afraid of what?"

She shrugged. "You tell me. Maybe—afraid of your father?" Her lips curled in a coy smile and her eyes searched his face and then looked deeply into his eyes, taunting him. Teasing him. Daring him.

Unable to meet her gaze, he looked away momentarily.

When he looked back, her eyes were still upon him. A shadow of a smile crossed her face. Her eyes mocked him. She moved closer, raising her eyebrows as if to say, "Well, are you with us?"

Joel's heart raced. He swallowed hard. "What time?"

"Three hours after sunset," Lank repeated, breaking the tension between Joel and the girl. "Be at the docks."

"Where is this...this tournament? What did you call it—the Dragon Tournament?"

"The Dragon Tournament is by invitation only," Lank replied mysteriously, "and thus its location is secret. Trust me, Joel—you'll have the time of your life! Now, are you with us or not?"

The girl's eyes seemed to bore into the depths of his soul.

Joel took a deep breath. "I'll be there."

Lank grinned and punched him playfully on the shoulder. "You're in for a wild time, my friend! See you at the docks."

The girl batted her eyes at him and gave him a seductive look. "Maybe I'll see you there, Joel." His heart raced when she said his name. And then, Lank and his companions were gone as quickly as they had come.

Joel moved away slowly, as if in a daze. There was a bitter taste in his mouth. He felt dizzy and nauseous. Never before had he deliberately gone behind his father's back, and he didn't like the feeling of betrayal that his decision brought now. For just an instant, the image of his father's face appeared in his memory but he shook his head and pushed it away.

He took a deep breath and let it out slowly. "Aye," he whispered, though there was no one within earshot. "I'll see you at the docks."

Chapter Five

A cool breeze rustled in the treetops as Joel opened the window of his sleeping loft and peered out. The night was dark, so dark he could barely see the tree beneath his window, yet his mind was made up. He took a deep breath and climbed through the window into the upper branches of the tree. A cold apprehension swept over him, a gnawing feeling of danger, but he pushed it aside. He would not back out—he would go to the Dragon Tournament with Lank.

He slid down the tree, and a thrill of adventure swept over him as his feet touched the ground. His conscience reproved him for his act of disobedience, but he ignored it. Pa would never know. He would only go to the Dragon Tournament this once. He paused beneath the front window, but all was dark and quiet. His departure had gone unnoticed.

The streets of Seawell were dark, so dark that he had to feel his way along. A dog began to bark and he walked faster, afraid that someone would come out to investigate. His heart pounded. His hands trembled. Everything within him seemed to shout, "Stop! Go back! Don't do this!" Shaking his head as if to quiet the voices within, he pushed ahead resolutely.

When he reached the docks his attention was immediately

drawn to a large, three-masted ship with a lantern hanging from the masthead. Two additional lanterns hanging above the ship's rail illuminated the dock. To his surprise, dozens of youth his age were strolling across the docks, laughing and jesting with each other as they headed for the vessel. Nearly two score were already aboard, laughing and talking together. Many held steins in their hands from which they sipped from time to time.

Joel stood in the shadows watching the activities. There was an air of festivity around the docks, but Joel was uneasy. Something didn't feel quite right. It was more than just the fact that he was doing this without his father's knowledge. In spite of the festive atmosphere, there was also an overriding premonition of danger, as if something dreadful was about to happen. Immense evil was present here; he could sense it.

I shouldn't be here, he told himself. *Pa trusts me. If he ever found out that I came here, I would lose that trust. I can't do this.* He turned to go back home.

"Joel," a voice greeted him, and he turned to find Lank at his elbow. "Glad you could come, my friend."

"I—I wouldn't miss it," Joel stammered.

"Well, let's go aboard."

"We're going by ship? Where is this Dragon Tournament, anyway?"

Lank shrugged. "I guess I can tell you now since you're here. It's on Elder Sister."

Joel was aghast. "The Isle of Dragons?"

Lank laughed. "Aye, of course. Where else would you expect to have a Dragon Tournament? Come on."

Joel held back. "Are these—are these real, live dragons?"

"Come on, Joel, don't be such a faint heart!" Lank growled impatiently. "We're about to miss the boat. Are you coming or not?"

At that moment, just one word would have kept Joel from making a disastrous decision. In his heart he knew he was making a wrong choice. If a friend had walked past and said, "Don't do it, Joel," he would have turned and run for home.

Instead, just the opposite happened. The girl he had seen outside the glass shop approached and laid a soft hand on his arm. "Joel, you remember Myra, don't you?" Lank said.

"Joel," Myra purred sweetly, "you're going with us, aren't you?"

And that was all it took. Without another thought Joel replied brightly, "Sure! Let's go."

As Joel and his companions reached the top of the gangway, a sailor met them with tall steins of ale. Lank and Myra each took one and Joel felt compelled to do the same. He really didn't want the drink and had no intention of consuming it, but he was afraid that his companions would mock him if he refused it. He carried it aboard, resolving to toss it overboard at the first opportunity.

The vessel got underway just moments later. The deck was crowded with young people, but the sailors managed to work around them as they cast off the mooring lines and readied the sails. Joel watched as the sails unfurled, billowing ghostly white against the darkness of the night. The vessel moved smartly out of the harbor and began to pound through the surf on her way to the island.

Still holding the stein of ale, Joel leaned against the rail and surveyed the scene before him. Scores of young men and women milled about on the upper deck of the ship, sipping occasionally from the tall steins in their hands, laughing and bantering with each other. Their language was revolting, almost as if they were vying with each other to see who could be the most profane. Some had obviously had far too much ale and struggled just to keep their footing on the swaying deck. Stewards passed among the throng, diligently keeping steins filled. A pall of evil hung over the scene and Joel suddenly felt very small, very alone, and very fearful. He was out of his element, and he knew it.

What am I doing here? he berated himself. *This is a death ship! All these people are headed for destruction and they don't even know it. Why did I ever let myself be talked into coming?* Glancing about to make sure that no one was watching, he flung the stein of ale over the rail and into the waves.

After a time the ship slowed and Joel looked forward to see that the ship was nearing the Twin Sisters. To Joel's astonishment, the vessel sailed into the channel between the two islands. Suddenly the decks swarmed with activity as the sailors furled the sails and prepared to dock. The ship glided into the secluded inlet and drifted to a stop. The sailors soon had the ship secured to the dock.

At that moment, fear swept across Joel's soul like a chilling north wind. *Pa's not afraid of anything or anyone,* he told himself, *yet he seemed almost terrified of this place! I wonder why? Is there something about this island that Pa knows and I don't? What is going to happen here tonight?*

He glanced up at the cliffs towering over the cove and was not surprised to see moving blue-white lights lining the stairs that ran to the top. In an instant he knew where he and the other youth were going. Just then he noticed that several other ships already rode at anchor in the cove.

A gangway was lowered from the side of the ship and the crowd of young people began to disembark. Separated from Lank and Myra, Joel found himself pushed along by a throng of eager revelers who laughed and chattered and drank greedily from their steins. As he stumbled down the gangway, the youth behind him prodded him in the back. "Can you move a little fasher, pal?" he slurred.

Irritated, Joel pushed back. "I can't go any faster than the people in front of me, dimwit." Reaching the end of the gangway, he stepped on the dock and then moved toward a narrow causeway of rugged ironshore. A well-worn trail led toward the cliffs.

Following the line of eager youth in front of him, Joel soon found himself climbing the stairs that led to the top of the cliffs. Glowing torches emitted a soft, blue-white light that illuminated the stairs. As he climbed higher, his feelings of anxiety gave way to sheer terror. *This is a place of great evil,* he told himself, *and something really bad is going to happen here tonight. Why did I come?* He considered stepping out of line and attempting to return to the ship, but somehow could not bring himself to even try. It was as if he were being pulled along by an unseen but powerful force that compelled him to stay in line with all the others.

The stairs entered the cleft in the mountainside, passed upward between two narrow shoulders of rock for fifty feet or so, and then came out on top of the cliffs. As Joel neared the brow of the cliff he became aware of a pounding rhythm surging upward like a blast of foul air, and he could hear the sounds of a large crowd. The iron stairs gave way to a rocky trail. When he reached the summit he stopped and stared in utter amazement.

He was standing on the brink of a vast stone amphitheater. Below him, hundreds and hundreds of flickering torches illuminated terraced rows of stone seats surrounding a huge, oval-shaped arena nearly two hundred yards across. The lowest rows of seats were already filled with hundreds of young people.

Burly guards at each side of the entrance were checking each of the young people, allowing them to enter only after they displayed some sort of pass. Joel panicked. *I don't have a pass!*

When it came Joel's turn, the guard looked at him sternly. "Your pass?"

"I—I don't have one," Joel stammered.

Lank stepped up at that moment. "He's with me." The guard nodded and let them enter.

As Joel followed the others down the stairs that led into the arena, he noticed that the far wall of the arena consisted of a row of cave-like openings closed off by large wooden gates. Rumbling growls and snarls emanated from behind the gates.

The line of eager youth filed past a cart loaded with tall earthenware steins. A man in an elegant robe was distributing them freely. Noticing that Joel had none, he thrust a stein into his hands. The look in the man's eyes told Joel that he was not about to take no for an answer. Joel's heart sank as he accepted the drink.

Joel followed Lank and Myra to the entrance of an elegant booth with plush seats. Joel's pulse quickened. *This is where the wealthy sit.* A guard stopped him. "This is a reserved area, lad," he said stiffly.

Lank waved the man aside. "He's with me." The guard nodded and stepped back.

As Lank and Myra took their seats Joel slid in beside them. Lank grinned at Joel. "You're gonna love this, Red."

The crowd was making so much noise that Joel missed Lank's comment entirely. "What did you say?"

"I said that you'll love this!" Lank repeated, leaning across Myra and raising his voice to be heard above the din.

Female servants passed through the crowd with trays of

drinks, their eyes scanning the crowd for any takers. They made trip after trip, for the crowd that night seemed exceptionally thirsty. When the drinks passed along the aisle in front of them, the girl on the other side of Lank took two steins. Joel noticed that there was no charge for the drinks.

Who pays for all this? he wondered. *We weren't charged passage on the ship and there was no admission charge to enter the amphitheater. And now they're passing ale out like water! Who is paying for all this?*

Drums began to beat in a slow, pulsing rhythm that reverberated throughout the arena, confusing and disorienting him. Joel could feel the heavy vibrations through his seat. His feelings of dread intensified. The vast crowd roared their approval, stamping their feet and swaying from side to side in perfect unison. The effect was as though the amphitheater itself was rocking like a fishing vessel in a storm. The noise was deafening.

Lank leaned across Myra. "The Dragon Tournament is about to start," he shouted above the roar.

Joel shouted back. "Lank, who's paying for all this?"

Lank shrugged. "Don't worry about it. It's always free."

The drums increased their tempo, beating faster and faster and faster until the arena trembled with expectancy. As sudden as the stroke of an axe, the drums were silenced. A score of trumpets sounded a rousing fanfare. The noisy horde of young people abruptly leaped to their feet. Startled, Joel stood up with them.

At the far end of the arena two huge brass gates opened slowly, majestically, and two lines of young people filed out and began to march proudly around the arena to the frantic cheers and screams of the waiting throng. Wearing chain mail shirts and helmets, the marching youth were arrayed in the brightest colors that Joel had ever seen. Each carried a tall banner that matched the colors in his clothing.

Lank leaned across Myra again. "These are the contenders in tonight's Tournament," he shouted.

The line of contenders reached the point where Joel and his companions stood. The crowd around Joel erupted with wild screams and cheers, stamping their feet, shaking their bodies, and putting their fingers to their mouths to emit shrill, ear-piercing whistles. Joel covered both ears. Lank noticed and laughed at him.

When the gaudy parade had made one complete lap around the amphitheater and received a thundering response from the crowd, the contenders disappeared again through the gates where they had entered. The gates slowly closed behind them. The vast throng of youth dropped to their seats and Joel imagined that they almost looked disappointed that the pageantry was over.

A lone drum began to beat with a slow, steady rhythm that made Joel cringe inside. He broke into a cold sweat. The cheering, swaying crowd, the pounding drum, the flickering torches—all worked together to create an atmosphere that un-nerved him. Evil was present here; he could feel it in the air.

His father's image seemed to appear before him and he re-coiled at the sight. *What would Pa say if he knew I was here?*

The wild cheering erupted again as the gates opened slight-ly and two colorful figures darted into the arena, one in bril-liant yellow carrying a long pike and the other in deep crimson bearing a heavy, two-handed sword that glittered in the torch-light. The tempo of the drum began to increase. The crowd abruptly fell silent. A roar of rage rumbled from some unseen place deep within the amphitheater.

"The contenders fight in teams of two tonight," Myra ex-plained to Joel. "These two contenders are regional champi-ons. They're good!"

"Who are they going to fight?" Joel asked.

Myra gave him a strange look. "The dragons, of course."

"Once the dragons are released into the arena," Lank expounded, "the contenders are awarded points for every second that they remain in the arena. They score ten contact points each time they strike the dragon with a weapon or twenty contact points should they manage to strike his head. A kill would score fifty points, although that happens very rarely."

Joel frowned. "Is it that hard to kill one?"

Myra gave him an incredulous look. "The dragons often win, you know."

"Win?" Joel gulped. "Do contestants actually get killed?"

Lank and Myra laughed. "They do if the referees can't get to them in time."

Joel was stunned. He studied the two contestants who stood awaiting the release of the first dragon. "These fellows are willing to go down there and fight a dragon, knowing all the time that they could get killed? Why? Why would they want to?"

"Do you know what a thrill it is to fight a dragon?" Lank asked, gazing at Joel as if he couldn't believe that he was having such a conversation. "They call it a rush. There's nothing like it."

Joel stared at Lank. "Have you ever competed in a Tournament?"

Lank grinned. "Of course." He pulled back his sleeve to reveal a long, jagged scar on his left forearm. "I was lucky I had a really fast referee."

Joel stared at the scar. "Would you ever fight again?"

Lank laughed. "Aye. Why wouldn't I? Like I said, there's nothing like it. It's a rush."

Joel shuddered. "What happens when a contender decides that he's had enough? How do you call off a dragon?"

"You don't," Lank replied. "See the little door at each end of the arena? There's another one just like those under the judges' stand across from us and a fourth one on our side that we can't see. The clock stops the moment either contestant makes it through one of those doors."

"What if you can't make it through in time? Do the dragons kill you?"

"That's where the referees come in," Lank explained. "Look—here they come now."

As he spoke, four helmeted men in chain mail armor strode proudly into the arena. Each carried a blazing torch at the end of an eight-foot pike. "When a contestant is down or disabled, the referees use their torches to drive the dragon back to its cage. Dragons are afraid of fire, you know."

"Afraid of fire?" Joel echoed. "I thought dragons breathe fire!"

Lank shook his head. "Only Cararian Greatwings and Nidian Swampfoots. These dragons are Slythian Pygmys."

"Pygmys? Are they smaller than other dragons?"

Lank nodded. "Adults only reach a maximum length of forty feet."

Joel puckered his lips. "Only forty feet. How much damage could a mere forty-foot dragon do?"

Myra touched his arm. "These may be young ones, but even they can be deadly."

Joel nodded. "I was jesting, Myra."

He glanced across the amphitheater and saw the judges' stand on the fourth row with six solemn robed figures sitting at it. Each had a parchment and a quill before him or her. As he watched, the official on the end stood to his feet with a large black cloth in his hand. He raised it in the air and then hurled it out into the arena. The crowd grew silent, tense with anticipation as the cloth drifted downward.

A thundering roar of rage blasted across the vast arena, echoing and re-echoing throughout the amphitheater until many of the spectators covered their ears in pain. Joel flinched, but Lank laughed. "Sounds like we've got a live one tonight."

As Joel watched in disbelief, one of the gates across the amphitheater flew open and a fifteen-foot dragon exploded into the arena. The huge beast ran to the center of the field, roaring in fury and swinging his massive head from side to side as if searching for a human to devour.

Joel trembled. The dragon was unlike anything that he had ever seen. Huge scaly legs supported a massive body covered in scales that looked as if they were fashioned from iron. The head was immense, with huge green eyes that smoldered with fury, and a cavernous mouth with teeth like daggers. The long, scaly tail whipped back and forth continuously like a serpent as the huge, batlike wings slowly opened and closed. The dragon's claws looked as if they could rip through the stoutest armor.

Joel held his breath without realizing it. The Dragon Tournament was about to commence. The dragon might be a young one, but Joel doubted that the two contenders would make it out of the arena alive.

Chapter Six

Joel glanced at the two young contenders and saw that both stood to one side of the arena, motionless. Puzzled, he turned to Lank and Myra. "What are they doing?"

"Trying for as many points as possible."

"Huh?"

"Contenders get one point for each second they stay in the arena with the dragon. Slythian dragons have a keen sense of smell, but very poor eyesight. They can see motion quite readily, so the two knights are standing still in hopes that the dragon cannot locate them for a few seconds."

"The dragons can readily see bright colors, so the Tournament Commission provides bright uniforms for the contenders," Myra chimed in. "Sorta gives the dragon a slight advantage, if you know what I mean."

The dragon stood motionless for a long moment as it scanned the arena, trying to determine the location of its adversaries. The four referees held their pike torches at the ready. Suddenly, with a scream of rage that reverberated throughout the amphitheater, the dragon charged across the arena. The two contenders stood their ground until the monster was almost upon them and then darted on both sides of it. The figure in yellow darted in close, jabbed the end of the pike up into the dragon's jaw, and then dashed around behind the beast. The crowd responded with a thunderous cheer. At that point, Joel saw to his amazement that the contender was female.

"Twenty points," Lank shouted in satisfaction.

"A girl?" Joel was incredulous. "The contender in yellow is a girl!"

"Is there anything wrong with that?" Myra demanded. "Girls like a little action, too."

"I—I just didn't expect to see a girl fight a dragon," Joel replied lamely.

The next twenty seconds held more excitement than most people experience in a lifetime. Joel watched in fascination as the daring young man and woman risked life and limb, darting in and out, striking the dragon and then retreating, moving so quickly that it seemed that the confused creature never quite knew from which direction the next attack would come. Working together, they managed to drive the beast back to the gate from which it came.

At that point the dragon stumbled and went down on one knee. As the girl distracted the creature, her partner ran right up the dragon's side and across its back. Lifting his sword with both hands, he attempted to drive it into the dragon's scaly head. The crowd roared its approval.

The enraged dragon shook its mighty head, hurling the youth to the sand. Before he could leap to his feet the dragon was upon him, pinning him to the ground with an enormous claw. The girl dashed in, stabbing at the dragon's face with her pike, but the beast swatted the weapon away every time. The dragon roared as it continued to crush the hapless youth beneath its claw. The crowd screamed. The resulting cacophony of noise rang throughout the amphitheater, overwhelming the senses.

Joel's heart was in his throat.

In an instant all four referees were on the scene, violently stabbing at the dragon with their long-handled torches. The creature retreated immediately. Waving their torches, the referees drove the dragon back into its cage, securing the gate behind it. A groan of disappointment went up from the crowd.

"Thirty-two seconds!" Lank exulted. "They were in the arena with the dragon for thirty-two seconds! Give them forty points for two blows to the head and then add in all the body blows—they had to have scored well over a hundred points!"

"How do you know they stayed thirty-two seconds?" Joel asked.

"I was counting."

"You were counting seconds during all that?" Joel shook his head. "I think I probably forgot to breathe during that round!"

Lank laughed.

An official at the judges' stand handed a small parchment to an aide who then went and posted the contenders' score on a large placard. "One hundred twelve," Myra read aloud. "That's one of the best scores I've ever seen."

The drum began to beat again and Joel's eyes darted immediately to the gates at the end of the arena. Two figures dressed in vivid green costumes accented with slashes of blue lightning slipped into the arena, one armed with a sword and one with a pike. Lank studied the uniforms. "I haven't seen this team battle before," he commented. "They must be new."

The black cloth was again tossed into the arena and a gate immediately crashed open. A dragon leaped into the arena, threw back its head, and roared in fury. The contenders took one look and then turned and dashed for the nearest exit.

The crowd responded with boos and hisses. Some even hurled
steins into the arena to vent their displeasure. Jeers and laughter rocked the amphitheater.

Joel laughed, and, without even thinking about what he
was doing, took a sip from his stein. "What was their time,
Lank?"

Lank snorted scornfully. "Three seconds, maybe?"

And so the Dragon Tournament continued. Joel sat wide-
eyed through round after round, watching in fascination as
brave but foolish youth risked their lives to make a name for
themselves or to provide sport for the others. Joel was surprised
at the large number of girls who participated. In some of the
rounds, contenders were injured, some seriously, but that fact
didn't seem to faze the Tournament participants or spectators.
In fact, Joel noticed that many of the spectators seemed to take
a fiendish delight in seeing their peers suffer. Without realizing
it, Joel drained three steins of ale during the event.

None of the contending teams that night came close to the
first score that was posted. Some posted scores in the seven-
ties and even in the eighties, but none reached the hundred
point mark.

As the final team of contenders strode into the arena wearing uniforms of gold and blue, Lank turned to Joel. "This team
is good. They were last year's champions."

"You'll notice that they both bear swords rather than the
usual sword and pike," Myra remarked. "They actually requested that of the Tournament Commissioners, though that places
them at a disadvantage. They're that good."

Joel nodded. He leaned forward in his seat, sipping contentedly at his stein of ale. Moments later he gasped as the dragon
burst into the arena. This was the largest and most ferocious
beast yet. Fully twenty feet long, it radiated rage as it tore

58

across the arena, violently thrashing its tail from side to side and screaming hideously.

Lank rubbed his hands together in anticipation. "Old Thaddeus," he said with a delighted grin. "Now here's some real action."

Joel stared at him. "Old Thaddeus?"

Lank nodded without taking his eyes from the furious dragon. "He's been around for a long time. He's the meanest of all the dragons. They say he's killed more contenders than all the other dragons put together."

"Really?" Joel shuddered as he studied the roaring dragon. "I'd hate to go into the arena with that thing."

Lank laughed. "Maybe someday you'll get that chance."

"I've been wondering something," Joel asked, changing the subject. "Why don't the dragons fly?"

"Their wings are clipped," Myra told him. "Otherwise, I suppose they would just fly away."

Roaring furiously, the dragon launched its attack on the two contenders. It leaped high into the air and then charged full speed toward the far end of the arena where the contenders waited. The youth did not wait for the huge dragon to engage them; they both raised their swords and charged it with lusty cries of exuberance.

Flapping its huge but useless wings, the dragon again leaped high into the air as it reached the contenders. To Joel's astonishment, both youth darted under the creature, leaping high to slash at its underbelly as they passed beneath it. The dragon roared in rage and pain. It spun around, dealing one of the contenders a glancing blow with its tail and knocking the helmet from his head. Joel was surprised when long, blond hair cascaded down around the contender's shoulders.

Joel turned to Myra. "It's another girl!"

The dragon reared back its head and emitted a cry that sounded like a woman shrieking in pain. Leaping high into the air again, it twisted its body around, using its tail to sweep the female contender off her feet. The huge beast landed on the girl and Joel feared that she had been crushed to death. Her companion rushed in, swinging his sword furiously as he drove the dragon backward. To Joel's amazement, the girl leaped to her feet, apparently unscathed, and rejoined her companion in the fray.

The amphitheater rocked with the raucous cheers of the crowd. Hundreds of voices began to chant the names of the two contenders. Others began to call, "Thaddeus! Thaddeus! Thaddeus!" and Joel was astounded to realize that they were cheering for the dragon.

Fearlessly the girl dashed toward the furious beast, swinging her sword with both hands in a valiant attempt to score against the creature. The dragon reversed direction at that instant, catching the contender with the side of his massive head and flinging her to the sand like a rag doll. In an instant he was upon her, pinning her to the sand with a sturdy foot.

With a mighty shout the male contender dashed toward the dragon in an attempt to save his partner. The dragon leaped forward, snatching the young man in its mighty jaws and flinging him toward the heavens. As the contender fell, arms and legs flailing, the beast caught him again in its mouth and shook him violently, much as a cat would shake a mouse. The youth's screams could be heard above the dragon's roaring.

The four referees dashed in with torches waving furiously. Lifting its head high, the dragon flung the limp body of the contender face down in the sand. Bellowing with rage, it lumbered to the door of its cage.

The girl in gold and blue knelt beside the body of her

companion, took one look, and then began to scream in anguish. The crowd began to chant, "Thaddeus! Thaddeus! Thaddeus!"

Lank turned to Joel with a nonchalant grin. "Well, Red, we lost one."

Joel stared at him for a moment, turned and looked at the lifeless form in the arena below, and then turned back to Lank. "You mean he's dead?"

Lank's grin widened. "As Myra said, sometimes the dragon wins."

Chapter Seven

"Joel! Wake up!" Pa's voice sounded hollow and distant as it forced its way through the fog and registered in Joel's consciousness. "You're late, Son."

Joel sat up and rubbed his eyes. His head throbbed painfully and his mouth felt scratchy and dry. He yawned, struggling to open his eyes.

"Joel!"

"I'm up, Pa." Joel forced his eyes open. The sleeping loft seemed hotter than usual. He felt dizzy and nauseous. If only the pounding in his head would stop. He reached for his shirt and then realized that he was already wearing it. Throwing back the covers, he stood to his feet. The room swayed a little.

He inhaled sharply as he thought about the dragons. Had he just dreamed it, or had he really been to the Dragon Tournament? His head continued to throb and he thought about the ale he had consumed. *So that's why I feel so sick.* Shame washed over him like a flood of putrid water. Never before had he tasted ale, for Pa had taught him about the evils of strong drink. *I'll never do that again,* he vowed.

"Joel! Your Ma has the vittles ready!"

"I'll be right down, Pa."

He reached for his clothes and then realized that he was already dressed, right down to his shoes. The pounding in his head increased until the room seemed to spin. He stood still for a long moment, breathing deeply and trying to clear his head. At last he started down the ladder, gripping the uprights desperately to keep from falling. He gave a sigh of relief when he reached the bottom safely.

"Son, you don't look so good."

Joel yawned and looked up. His mother was just setting two bowls of porridge on the table. "I'm all right, Ma."

"You don't look 'all right.' Didn't you sleep well?"

He shrugged. "I slept fine," he replied, and then realized that he had just lied to his mother.

Wynn and Cobby were already at the table. "You do look rough," Wynn told Joel. "Son, are you going to survive?"

Joel took his seat at the table. "That's about all I'm going to do," he muttered. He stared at his bowl of porridge. *I think I'd rather sleep than eat breakfast.* His head throbbed.

Wynn sent a petition of thanks to King Emmanuel and then the family began their meal. "Let's fish the eastern side of Elder Sister today," Cobby told Wynn. "If the cod aren't running, perhaps the blues will be."

Wynn nodded. "Sounds good to me."

"I heard a couple of mothers talking at the market yesterday," Ruth told Cobby as the meal progressed. "It seems that many of the youth of Seawell are going to the Dragon Tournaments on Elder Sister. Cobby, they're having the Tournaments every Friday night now!"

Cobby nodded. His face was grim. "These youth don't know what they're getting into, Ruth. They're playing with fire and don't realize how badly they're going to get burned. They're going to have their lives destroyed, but they won't realize it until it is too late."

He shook his head sadly. "It seems that these lads will do anything for a thrill, even if it kills them."

"It's not just the boys, though, Cobby," Ruth interjected. "I hear that the girls are going in as great numbers as the boys, and that they're even participating in the Tournaments. Imagine—a girl fighting a dragon! In my day, a young lady wouldn't have thought of such a thing."

"Why don't the parents put a stop to this foolishness?" Wynn asked. "What's wrong with parents these days?"

"Most of them don't have control of their families," Cobby replied. "And I suppose that some of the parents don't even know that their youth are involved."

Wynn snorted. "Have parents stopped being parents?" He looked questioningly at Joel. "What have you heard about the Dragon Tournaments? Is this something the young people talk about?"

Joel shrugged, trying to look nonchalant, though his face burned and his heart pounded as if he had been running up a steep hill. "I—I guess I haven't heard them talk much about it." He dropped his eyes and looked at his bowl.

Cobby frowned. "I wish there was something we could do to keep the young people from the island. They're in greater danger than they realize."

Wynn spooned more porridge into his bowl. "At least we don't have to worry about Joel. He knows better than to go to the Tournaments. Right, Joel?"

Joel nodded, but his heart constricted with fear. *He doesn't know—surely he doesn't know!* He studied Papa Wynn's face, trying to determine if his grandfather suspected anything. But the old man's countenance was open and relaxed and Joel decided that he did not.

Joel was relieved when the conversation turned to another topic.

When breakfast was finished, Cobby turned to his father. "Let's you and I get the *Princess* ready while Joel goes to get fresh salt for the hold. We should have been out on the banks an hour ago."

⁂

Joel stumbled along the canal street of Seawell, struggling to keep his eyes open. His head still throbbed and every muscle in his body ached. He took a deep breath and let it out slowly, wishing he could have just stayed in bed. *This is going to be a long day,* he told himself ruefully. *I shouldn't have let myself be talked into going to the Dragon Tournament.* He kicked a stone along the street. *I have to admit, though, it was the most exciting thing I have ever seen.*

"Hey, Red," a voice called, and Joel turned to see Marcus and Dade approaching from a side alley. "Saw you at the Tournament last night, Red. You were really putting the ale away!" Both laughed.

Joel's heart lurched. *I don't even know these fellows,* he thought in dismay. *What if this gets around town? What if it gets back to Pa?* He shrugged. "The Tournament was all right, I guess. Could have used a bit more action, though."

"More action?" Marcus echoed. "Didn't you see Leonard get killed? How much more action do you want?"

"Are you coming next Friday night?" Dade asked.

Joel shrugged. "I don't know."

"You really ought to come," Marcus urged. "There's going to be free ale again. It will be quite a night."

Joel stared at him. *Usually these fellows won't even talk to me,* he told himself. *Now they're acting like they really want me at the Tournament.* "I'll have to see how busy I am that night," he replied. "I'll come if I can."

"Well, we hope you can make it," Dade remarked.

Joel's mind was in turmoil as he walked away. *I've already decided that I'm not going back to the Tournament,* he told himself, *but Lank and Marcus and Dade seem to really want me there. Maybe this is a chance to have some real friends.*

And Myra... His heart leaped as he thought of the slender girl with the dark hair and the cheerful laugh. Sure, she was with Lank, but her eyes told Joel that she was interested in him. If he went to the Tournament, Myra would be there...

He sighed. *What would Pa say if he knew? And Papa Wynn... How can I do this behind their backs?*

The *Princess* was ready to sail when he reached the dock. "Come on, lad, we're about to leave without you," Cobby called. Joel leaped aboard as the two men pushed the cog away from the dock. Wynn hoisted the sail with Cobby at the tiller and the harbor was soon left behind them.

Deep in thought, Joel sat on the nets as the *Princess* bounded eagerly toward blue water. *What if I go to the Dragon Tournament but don't drink the ale?* he asked himself. *What would be wrong with that?*

"What's on your mind?" Cobby called, with a friendly grin. "You look like you're in another world."

Joel shook his head. "I'm all right, Pa. I'm just tired."

Joel wrestled all week with the Dragon Tournament temptation. He told himself repeatedly that he would not go again, that he would not betray his father and grandfather, and that it really didn't matter what the other youth in town thought of him. But try as he might, he could not get away from one simple fact: the Tournament was a point of contact with other youth his age. If he went, he was part of the group and would be accepted by them; if he chose not to go he would be on the outside looking in. Attendance at the Dragon Tournament was an opportunity to make friends, a chance to be accepted.

On Friday afternoon Cobby let him take the tiller and bring the *Princess* into the harbor on the return from the day's fishing. "Take it all the way to the dock," he instructed. "You're handling her like an old salt now."

Joel hesitated. "Are you sure?"

Cobby grinned. "Would I let you take her in if I didn't think you were ready for it? Son, I trust you. Take her all the way in to the dock."

"Aye, sir." Joel tried unsuccessfully to hide the proud grin that threatened to display itself. "Thank you, sir."

Joel stood in the stern, watching the afternoon sun sparkling on the waves, listening to the screech of gulls, the creaking of the mast and the flutter of the sail, and smelling the salt air. He watched his father for a moment. *Cobby of Seawell might be just a fisherman to most, but he's the greatest man I know. And to think he trusted me with the tiller of the Princess!*

His heart smote him as he thought about the Dragon Tournament. *I won't go tonight,* he sternly told himself. *I won't let Pa down. He trusts me, and I won't do anything to lose that! Knowing that Pa trusts me is more important than making friends with Lank and his gang, anyway.*

He leaned into the tiller and brought the *Princess* into a sweeping turn to starboard. The cog entered the harbor and glided past the various fishing craft. "Ready with the sail?" he sang out.

"Ready for your order, sir," Cobby replied, standing at the masthead.

"Sails down, now!" Joel called, and the sail came tumbling down as his father released it.

The *Princess* glided easily into her berth and nudged against the dock as gently as a kitten nuzzling its mother. Wynn secured the bow line while Joel secured the stern. "Perfect!" Cobby called. "There's not a man in Seawell that could have done it better."

Joel grinned. "I've sailed and trained under the best captain in these parts, sir."

Cobby laughed.

Wynn stood at the hold and prepared to sort through the day's catch. "Like father, like son, I always say."

Cobby nodded happily. "Son, I'm proud of you."

Joel leaped to the dock. "I'll get the cart." As he hurried up the street, he saw a raven-haired girl approaching. "Myra!"

Myra looked up at him. "Will I see you at the Dragon Tournament tonight, Joel?"

He took a deep breath and let it out slowly. "Not tonight, Myra."

She gave him a coy look and her lips seemed to pout. "Why not, Joel? I was really hoping you would go with me."

"What would it matter, Myra? You'll be with Lank, anyway."

She touched his arm and a warm thrill went through his soul like a spark of electricity. "That's not the same. You're the one I want to be with."

He tilted his head. "Does Lank know that?"

She stared at him with huge eyes and his heart pounded faster. "Lank is my next-door neighbor, Joel. That's all. There's nothing special between us." She caressed his arm. "You're the one I want to be with. The Dragon Tournament won't be the same without you."

"I can't go, Myra. I just can't."

A hurt look swept across the girl's face and she actually

looked as if she might cry. "Please, Joel. You've got to go."

His resolve melted in an instant. "I—I guess one more night won't hurt anything," he stammered. "I'll see you tonight at the docks."

She smiled. "You've made me one happy girl, Joel. See you tonight." She hurried away.

Weeks went by, and Joel found himself sneaking out of the house every Friday night to attend the Dragon Tournaments. Attendances soared as the youth from other regions began to find their way to the island. The event itself was thrilling enough, for the opportunity to watch your peers fight live dragons was an experience not soon to be forgotten. Joel enjoyed the camaraderie that was developing between himself and the other youth of Seawell; for the first time in his life he felt accepted. He was becoming one of them. He found himself drinking larger and larger quantities of ale during the Tournament, for the beverage was free and the supply was abundant. But his real delight was seeing Myra. As thrilling as the dragon battles were, he found himself watching her instead of the action in the arena.

But his relationship with his father suffered. An overwhelming weight of guilt seemed to settle on his chest every time he saw his father and thought of his own deceit and duplicity.

Time after time he resolved to stop attending the Tournament, even if it meant that he would also have to stop seeing Myra, but he never could quite bring himself to go through with his decision. Week after week he found himself making the journey to Elder Sister and then hating himself the next day.

"Tonight will be a Tournament like no other," Lank told him mysteriously one afternoon. "You'll remember this night for a long time to come."

"What's so different about tonight?" Joel responded. "It's not my first Tournament, you know."

"Tonight," Lank announced grandly, "one of the contenders is none other than Joel of Seawell!"

"Joel of—" the young fisherman began, and then realized what he was saying. "Lank, that's preposterous! I've never fought a dragon in my life!"

Lank grinned, a slow, irritating grin that rankled Joel. "Tonight you will, my friend."

"Lank, I am not going down into that arena, so forget that idea once and for all. I'm not about to fight a dragon."

The older youth grinned at him. "Hey, it will be a chance to impress Myra."

Joel grinned. "I can't say that I wouldn't welcome that, but seriously, Lank, I've been thinking more and more about dropping the Tournaments altogether. I have to sneak out of the house every time I go, and I really don't like doing things behind my father's back. If Pa ever found out, it would kill him."

"All right, I can understand that," Lank said slowly, nodding his head as he spoke. "I tell you what, Joel—I'll make a deal with you. Fight in the Tournament tonight with me, and I'll never again ask you to go to another Tournament. Fair enough?"

"Promise?" Joel asked.

"Of course."

"Say it."

"I promise."

"All right, but I'm still not ready to fight a dragon."

Lank chuckled. "It's not as hard as it seems," he assured Joel. "You'll do just fine. Besides, I'll be your partner. You and I will do well together."

"What if we draw Old Thaddeus?" Joel protested. "I'm not about to get into an arena with that killer! Three times now I've seen him kill a contender. Three times, Lank."

"Contenders have the right to turn down the dragon they draw," Lank assured him. "It can cost serious points, but you can do that if you want to bad enough. If we draw Old Thaddeus we'll just request another draw."

Joel nodded, but a cold fear crept across him like a cancer. He knew he wasn't prepared to fight a live dragon, but he lacked the courage to refuse Lank and so he simply acquiesced. "All right. If you'll go into the arena with me, I'm game. I'll fight a dragon."

It was a decision that Joel would regret.

Chapter Eight

Joel and Myra stood at the rail, watching as the ship sailed into the moonlit cove of Elder Sister. Joel was astounded to see that a number of large ships rode at anchor in the secluded inlet. He turned to Lank, who loitered a short distance away. "What are all these ships doing here?"

Lank grinned his usual toothy grin. "Tonight is a very special Tournament," he replied. "Tonight contenders from all over the kingdom will compete. This will be the largest event you have ever seen."

"They look like warships," Myra commented. "What would warships be doing here?"

"Actually, they look more like slave galleys," Joel replied.

Lank laughed. "Will you two lighten up? These ships are designed to carry large numbers of people, for there will be thousands at the Dragon Tournament tonight. As I said, this will be an event like no other."

"And I agreed to compete in the arena," Joel muttered.

"You're gonna do just fine," Lank assured him. "I've fought dragons numerous times and I can tell you this—there's nothing to it. As long as we stay together we'll both do fine."

Joel glanced down at the stein in his hand. Just now it didn't seem like a good idea. "Other contenders have been killed, Lank."

"Only because they made mistakes. Trust me, Joel, there's nothing to worry about."

The ship was now secured at the dock and the gangway dropped into place. The youthful passengers pushed and shoved in their eagerness to disembark. Myra tugged at Joel's arm. "Let's go, tall boy. I can't wait to see tonight's action."

Lank put a hand on Joel's shoulder, momentarily restraining him. "One more thing. There will be rum tonight along with the usual ale. Don't drink any until after our round in the arena."

"Huh?"

"You don't want to be drunk when you're facing a dragon."

Joel laughed. "Nay, I guess not."

The crowd surged forward, sweeping Joel and Myra along with them. Joel could not have backed out if he wanted. Moments later he and Myra were climbing the iron stairs up the face of the cliff with everyone else. His heart pounded. This was to be a night of thrills and excitement, a night to remember, and yet, deep inside, a voice was warning him that there was danger ahead. The uneasy feeling persisted all the way to the amphitheater entrance.

Lank caught up with them at the gates. "Follow me," he told Joel. "I'll show you the way backstage where we will prep for our round."

Joel glanced back at him and was bewildered by what he saw. On each side of the massive entrance gate, fully a dozen burly knights in chain mail stood at attention. Their helmets were in place as if they were prepared for battle, and each clutched a pike. Their faces were hard and their eyes seemed filled with hatred as they watched the youthful revelers.

Joel was uneasy. Something was wrong here, dreadfully wrong, but he wasn't sure exactly what it was. For some unexplained reason, he suddenly found himself desperately longing for the company of his father. "L-Lank," he said, trying to keep his voice from betraying him, "why are there so many guards tonight?"

"There are guards at every Tournament," Lank replied smoothly. "They're here to make sure that no one gets hurt."

"But there have never been this many," Joel persisted. "There are more than a score at this one gate alone!"

"This is the largest Tournament we're ever had," Lank told him. "I suppose that there is a need for more security." He started down into the arena. "Come on, or we'll be late. See you, Myra."

The ominous feeling of impending disaster persisted, but Joel nodded and followed Lank. "I suppose so."

Ten minutes later, after the introductory lap around the arena, Joel and Lank stood behind the huge brass gate, clad in bright uniforms of red, yellow, and green. A Tournament official approached them carrying a sword and a pike. "Choose your weapon," Lank told him. "Which are you most comfortable with?"

"I haven't really handled either," Joel replied nervously, "but I suppose I'll take the pike."

"Hey—relax!" Lank told him, handing him the pike and taking the sword for himself. "Just stay with me and we'll be fine. The only thing you have to remember is this—once the dragon charges us, keep moving. Stay close to him, but keep moving. Go for the eyes, the throat, or the belly; everything else is covered with armored scales."

"The eyes, the throat, or the belly," Joel repeated. "Got it."

The drum increased in tempo and the gate began to move.

Lank grinned at him. "Ready for this?"

"Not really!" Joel exclaimed. "Why are we the first contenders tonight?"

"It was the luck of the draw," Lank returned. "Ready? Stay with me!" With these words, he slipped from behind the gate and dashed across the arena. Joel had no choice but to follow.

Joel ran into the arena to an explosive cacophony of sound. The drum was booming so loudly that he could actually feel the concussions inside his head. The crowd roared and he looked up into the stands to realize that every seat was filled; there were thousands of youth in attendance tonight. This was indeed the largest Dragon Tournament he had ever seen.

The sand beneath his feet was thick and dry and made running difficult. During the introductory lap he had quickly discovered that slogging through it was like running with weights fastened to his feet. *This will add to the danger,* he now told himself. *It will make it more difficult to outmaneuver the dragon.*

Lank was twenty yards ahead of him, so he sprinted hard to catch up. As he ran he glanced up into the stands, trying to catch a glimpse of Myra. The crowd cheered him. Deciding to make the most of the moment, he held the pike high with both hands and grinned at the crowd as he ran. The amphitheater echoed with the roar of approval.

At that moment he ran full speed into Lank, who had stopped. The impact sent them both to their knees in the sand. The amphitheater rang with laughter. Lank snarled, "Watch where you're going, you idiot!"

The thousands of spectators began to laugh and to jeer, and Joel was humiliated. His embarrassment was forgotten in an instant when he saw the Tournament official stand to his feet with a black cloth in his hand. *This is it,* he thought desperately.

The cloth fluttered into the arena and an instant hush settled over the crowd.

Joel suddenly realized that he was standing less than fifty yards from the nearest emergency exit. All he had to do was dash through the doorway and the round would be over. He and Lank wouldn't score any points, but they would still be alive. Lank seemed to read his thoughts. "Run for the exit and I'll cut you down like a cur dog," he growled. "And don't think I wouldn't do it."

At that moment a gate slammed open and a dragon exploded into the arena. Terror swept over Joel, rendering him unable to move, to breathe, or to think. The dragon was enormous. Scaly legs as thick as trees supported a massive body covered in gray scales that appeared to be made of iron. The head was massive, with huge golden eyes that smoldered with fire and a cavernous mouth with teeth like daggers. The long, scaly tail whipped back and forth continuously like a serpent as the huge, batlike wings slowly opened and closed. The dragon's claws looked as if they could rip through the stoutest armor. The beast reeked of death and dismemberment.

"Stand still until he sees us and attacks," Lank said in a low voice. "And once he attacks, don't stop moving. If you can get close to him and stay close to him, always running around him, it seems to confuse him."

The dragon crept forward with a low growl rumbling in its throat. The massive head swept slowly from side to side and Joel realized that the deadly beast had not yet located them. His heart pounded and his breath came in short, ragged gasps. The blood pounded in his head so loud that he could no longer hear the roar of the crowd. His chest constricted and his limbs trembled. Overwhelmed with terror, he dropped his head and slowly became aware of the fact that a pike was lying at his feet. *My pike!* he thought numbly, staring at it until it finally occurred to him to pick it up. He knelt to retrieve the weapon.

At that instant the dragon spotted him and charged across the arena with an ear-shattering roar of rage. "Come on!" Lank cried, running forward to engage the beast.

Joel ran after Lank, although his senses screamed for him to run in the other direction. Lank charged directly at the dragon and then at the last possible moment darted to one side, circling behind the creature. Bellowing with rage, the dragon turned to follow Lank.

Lank darted under the beast from behind, slashing upward at the great belly. The dragon immediately dropped, crushing Lank to the sand. Only Lank's head, arm, and shoulder protruded from beneath the great bulk of the beast. The dragon thrashed from side to side in an attempt to crush the life out of the hapless contender beneath him. "Help me, Joel!" Lank cried in desperation. "This monster is trying to crush me!"

Without hesitation Joel dashed forward to save his partner. He ran right up the dragon's shoulder and stabbed at the great golden eye, one of the beast's most vulnerable spots. The blow fell short and the point of the pike struck the fleshy part of the cheek, just below the eye. The beast flinched, roaring in pain, and Joel knew that he had found a tender spot. He leaped up again, striking the dragon again in the very same spot.

With a scream of rage that reverberated across the vast amphitheater like a crash of thunder, the great beast rolled away from Joel, freeing Lank in the process. The referees ran in with their blazing torches, driving the bellowing beast away from the downed contender. Lank scrambled to his feet, apparently unhurt. The referees backed off and the round continued.

"Thanks, Joel," Lank gasped. "He nearly finished me."

The dragon came charging in at that moment and the battle

continued. For the next fifteen seconds the great beast and the two young contenders gave the vast audience a performance they would never forget. Darting in and out, always circling the ponderous beast, Lank and Joel managed to avoid the sharp claws and menacing jaws.

And then it happened. The dragon lunged for Lank, and Joel leaped in, stabbing at the beast's great soft underbelly. But Joel had underestimated the dragon's cunning. The creature twisted to one side, swinging his mighty tail in a wide arc that slammed Joel against the rocky embankment. The pike went flying. In an instant the dragon was upon him, crushing his hips and legs to the sand with a powerful foot. "Lank!" Joel cried. "Help me!"

As the crowd roared with excitement, Joel caught a glimpse of the emergency door closing behind Lank. His partner had deserted him. Unless the referees could get to him in time, his life was about to end.

Reaching as far as he could, he managed to grasp the pike. He twisted his upper body, thrusting the sharp point of the pike over his shoulder and penetrating the soft tissue between the dragon's toes. A roar of rage assaulted his ears, but the crushing pressure on his lower back and legs was gone in an instant. He dropped the pike and rolled underneath a ledge of rock.

The dragon roared and clawed at the ledge, determined to get at the terrified contender. One huge foot raked the length of the ledge and two sharp claws slashed the side of Joel's leg, slicing his thigh open. He screamed in pain and slid his body as tight as he could against the back of the crevice. Roaring horribly, the furious dragon clawed at the ledge again and again. Dirt and rocks fell down upon Joel as the frenzied dragon dug at the ledge.

Joel was terrified. *Where are the referees?* he thought as he watched the deadly claws repeatedly pass within inches of his body. With each pass they came a little closer as the frenzied beast dug away at his hiding place. *Why don't the referees do something?*

Suddenly the deadly claws were gone and a booted foot appeared at the edge of the ledge. *The referees! They're here at last!* Weak with fear, Joel managed to crawl from beneath the ledge before blacking out.

When he awoke he found himself lying on his back. He lifted his head and took a look at his thigh, recoiling at the sight that met his eyes. His leg was wrapped in a dirty, blood-soaked cloth bandage. Pain coursed through his body.

"Here," an attendant said, handing him a metal cup. "Drink this. It will kill the pain."

Joel took a sip and then gagged on his first taste of rum. The attendant laughed. "Choke it down," he urged. "When the pain really starts you'll be glad you did."

Joel blacked out again.

When he awoke the second time he was astounded to realize that he was back in the stands and that the Tournament was proceeding as usual. Myra was bending over him. "Joel, are you all right?"

"The leg hurts quite a bit," he told her, "but I guess I'll live."

"The dragon nearly killed you," she told him, and her eyes shone with a light he had never seen before. "They say you lost a lot of blood. You nearly died, Joel."

Joel was light-headed and dizzy. Myra's face seemed to swim in and out of focus. "I need to rest," he said. "I don't feel too good." He lay down and closed his eyes.

When he awoke again Myra helped him to a sitting position and then handed him a stein. "You won't believe it," she gushed. "They have free rum tonight!" She giggled. "I shuppose I have already had more than my share."

Joel stared at her. The girl was already half-drunk and slurring her words. He took a cautious sip of the rum and found it disagreeable, so he placed the stein on the seat beside him.

The drum began to beat with a strange, irregular tempo. "What's happening?" Joel asked Myra.

"They just finished a round," she replied, "and we're waiting for the next round to begin."

The drum stopped abruptly and an unearthly hush fell over the vast amphitheater. All eyes darted to the arena as a tall, broad-shouldered knight in chain mail strode briskly across the sand and stopped in the center. "Lend me your ear," he cried in a powerful voice that rang across the vastness of the amphitheater. "We want all of you to come down to the arena. We will give you the opportunity to meet tonight's contenders. Please make your way down the stairs at this time. Attendants will help you into the arena."

The huge crowd stood to their feet. Attendants began sliding back sections of the low walls separating the arena from the seating galleries. Laughing and chattering, the crowd began to flow down into the arena and across the sand like a wave of the sea. Joel noticed that many of them staggered and had trouble walking. He watched the faces of the youths passing his seat and was appalled at what he saw. Eyes wide and staring, mouths agape, and faces devoid of any expression, the revelers moved forward as if controlled by some force beyond themselves.

Joel looked at Myra and saw the same vacant stare. "Myra! Are you all right?" She turned to him, her lips moving as if struggling to form words, but no sound was coming forth. *It's the rum,* he realized in panic. *There was something in the rum to incapacitate everyone! We have to get out of here!*

He stood to his feet, gritting his teeth against the burning pain that coursed through his injured leg. "Myra, follow me," he said quietly. "I don't know what's happening, but we have to get out of here." *And am I glad I didn't drink much of the rum!*

Myra started forward but Joel held her back. "No, Myra, let's go out the back way. I think this is some kind of a trap." He turned her toward the gates at the top of the arena but a burly guard met them in the aisle.

"Move along with everyone else," he ordered.

"My friend isn't feeling well," Joel protested. "I want to get her out some place where she can rest."

"No one's feeling well right about now," the guard replied with a vicious grin. "Just move along as you're told. No one leaves by the back exits."

The drum sounded just once, a loud crash that echoed across the vast arena and grabbed the attention of the revelers. "Keep moving toward the center of the arena," the knight in chain mail ordered in a compelling voice. "Make room for those be-hind you. Keep moving until everyone is in the arena."

When Joel and Myra and the last of the confused youth were inside the arena, the attendants slid the movable sections back into place, sealing off the arena. Apprehension knotted in Joel's stomach like a fist. He studied the faces of those around him, realizing that not one showed any signs of alarm. *They move like mindless creatures,* he told himself, *just doing as they are* told. *Whatever was put in the rum is working well.*

He pulled Myra closer to him. *I don't know what is going to happen, but I know it's not going to be good. There has to be some way out of here.*

The drums began to beat a fast, frantic rhythm, and Joel realized that the sound had a hypnotic, controlling effect. He struggled against it. At that moment, scores of burly guards moved into the arena and began to pass among the throngs of young revelers. Joel heard the metallic clank of heavy chains. As he watched in horror, he saw that the guards were snapping leg irons on each of the youth, chaining them together in lines of twelve.

His mind raced. Suddenly he could visualize the large ships riding at anchor in the cove and in an instant he realized what was happening. His mind reeled at the thought and his very soul cried out against it. "Those are slave galleys in the cove," he told Myra. "We're being taken as slaves!"

At that moment a guard grabbed Myra, forcing her ankles into leg irons and dragging her over to be chained with a group of other young females. Joel knew that he was powerless to help. Another guard grabbed him, and in moments he also was wearing leg irons and was shackled in a line of young men. "Myra!" he called in desperation as the group of captive girls was led away. Myra disappeared into the crowd of helpless young slaves.

Ten minutes later, as Joel and his companions were led from the arena, they chanced to pass within a few feet of Lank, who stood to one side, triumphantly watching the proceedings. "You betrayed us, Lank!" Joel spat out the words. "You wretched snake, you betrayed us!"

Lank grinned. "You made it so easy," he replied glibly. "You were so gullible."

A tall, well-muscled warrior in chain mail approached just then, and as Lank saluted, Joel realized that he was a warlord from another land. "Everything went as planned, Captain," Lank said proudly. "I'm delivering nearly two hundred youth from Seawell into your hands, sire."

The tall captain stepped back and looked Lank over as if sizing him up. "I suppose some of your friends and family members are among the captives?"

"Aye, sire," Lank replied, drawing himself up to his full height. "Many of them are."

"A man who will betray family and friends is worthless to me," the captain said coldly, "for he cannot be trusted." With these words, he drew a dagger and plunged it into Lank's heart. An expression of utter amazement crossed Lank's face as he fell to the floor and died.

Joel trembled uncontrollably, limping along in the line of captives as they followed the iron stairs down toward the waiting galleys. The pain in his injured leg was agonizing. The shackles chafed his ankles and the chains rattled with every step. His heart ached. When the line of slaves reached a certain vantage on the face of the cliff, for just an instant he could see the lights of Seawell. *I'll never see my home again,* he thought bitterly. *Never again will I ever hear Pa's voice or feel Ma's gentle hand on my shoulder. Never again will I see Papa Wynn's encouraging smile.*

The tears flowed freely, blurring his vision as he struggled across the cold sands of the secluded cove.

Chapter Nine

The stench in the lower hold of the slave galley was unbearable. Chained to an oar between two other lads, Joel fought against a rising sense of panic. For three long days and nights he had sat on the narrow bench, rowing for hours at a time, catching what sleep he could in the brief rest periods that were allowed between rowing sessions. Water had been rationed out several times a day, but the two meals a day consisted merely of a small piece of hard biscuit known as hardtack and a piece of dried and heavily salted fish.

Chained to the oars as they were, the captives were not even allowed breaks to attend to personal needs. Joel felt dirtier than he had ever felt in his life.

He thought of Myra. Were the female slaves being treated any better than this? He doubted it. His heart went out to her and he wondered if he would ever see her again. *Will I ever see Seawell again, or Ma or Pa or Papa Wynn?*

The hold was dark, oppressive, and like a prison. *Where are they taking us?* he wondered. *We've been traveling for three days now before a strong wind. How far are we from home?* As he rowed he stared around the hold at the other young slaves. Nearly two hundred young men rowed in unison to the cadence of the relentless drum. Any slowing or slacking quickly brought the stinging lash from the whip of one of the guards.

His leg throbbed. The wounds were dark and angry and he feared that they were becoming infected. He had no way to bathe the wounds or attend to them in any way. Clenching his teeth against the pain he rowed harder, for one of the guards was moving in his direction.

Why could I not see that Lank was not really my friend? he asked himself bitterly. *He set a trap for me and I walked right into it! How could I have been so blind? How could I have been so foolish?*

The drum abruptly ceased its throbbing and with deep sighs of relief the young slaves released their grip on the oars. Rest periods were too few and far between, and certainly much too brief. Joel turned to the lad on his left. "Micah, how are your blisters?" he asked in a low whisper.

Micah looked at his tortured hands. "Two of the blisters have torn open now. I'm not sure how much more of this I can take." He glanced downward. "How is your leg doing?"

Joel shook his head. "Not too well, I'm afraid. I'd give anything to have my ma clean it and dress it." Suddenly he found himself blinking back tears, but Micah pretended not to notice.

Jared, the young slave to Joel's right, spoke up. "Hey—I just realized something! You were a contender at the Tournament, weren't you?" He eyed Joel's uniform, though it was bloodied and soiled almost beyond recognition. "Were you the one who was trapped under the ledge by the dragon?"

Joel nodded.

"What was it like? What was it like to participate in the Dragon Tournament?" Jared's eyes were wide with awe.

Joel just shook his head. "Let's not even talk about it." He sighed heavily. "I just wish I knew where we are going."

"Don't you know?" Micah replied to this. "We're sailing to Corthia."

"Corthia?" Joel echoed. "How do you know?"

"What's Corthia?" Jared interrupted.

"Corthia is one of the largest and wealthiest city-states in all of Terrestria," Micah told Jared. "It's more than a thousand nautical miles from Seawell. The Corthians are proud of the fact that it takes a full day's travel to cross the city. It's said that more than a million people live there."

Jared shook his head. "That's one enormous city!"

Joel turned to Micah. "How do you know we're going to Corthia?"

"Well, I don't know it for sure, of course, but I'm pretty sure. This is a Corthian ship, you know."

"How do you know that?"

"There's the Corthian symbol right there on the forward bulkhead." Micah pointed to a large, blue emblem of a bird with wings outstretched. "That's the Corthian war bird. You'll see it on the soldiers' shields as well."

"And so you figure we're going to Corthia," Joel said.

Micah shrugged. "It makes sense. We're sailing east on a Corthian ship. Corthia is known for their extensive slave trade. Where else would we be going?"

"What will happen to us when we get there?" Jared asked.

"If we're simply being taken as slaves, we'll be sold at public auction. Of course, there are fates worse than slavery."

Joel's heart constricted. "Such as...?"

Micah grimaced. "Being sacrificed in the temples to the Corthian deities."

Joel gulped. "They actually do that?"

Micah nodded grimly. He reached up for the gourd dipper of water being proffered by a servant, took the biggest gulp he could get away with, and then passed the gourd to Joel. "They sacrifice a certain number of slaves from each foray. It could very well be one of us."

"How do you know all this about the Corthians?" Jared asked.

"My father is a merchant of Corthian silk," Micah replied. "He's had dealings with them for a number of years."

The drum began to beat again and two hundred pairs of hands immediately reached for the oars, for the slightest delay would be rewarded with the stinging lash of the whip. Joel and his companions fell silent and commenced rowing.

Two days later the ship stopped at the edge of a small bay. When the drum signaled a rest break Joel leaned forward and rested his head on the oar. "I'm about to die."

"Pay attention!" a voice barked, and the slaves looked up to see the cadence officer standing amidships. "The captain says that the ship stinks because of you. He wants you all overboard! Now pay attention. When we release you from your chains, follow the slave in front of you. You will go up on deck, jump over the rail, and swim to the rope ladders hanging down amidships. If you cannot swim, grab a line and pull yourself to the ladders. Once you are back aboard you will make your way back to the rowing station where you are now. Any rower who cannot find his place will receive ten lashes, so make sure you know where you are right now."

He stopped and glared at the rowers. "We will have archers on the fore and aft decks. Should one of you be so foolish as to attempt an escape, we will fill your carcass with arrows before you even know what happened. Now, let's see how well you listened."

Four soldiers with keys came through the ranks of rowers, unlocking the torturous leg irons and allowing the prisoners to move from their oars. Row after row, the weary rowers followed their tormentors topside.

Joel limped up the stairs, biting his lip against the resulting pain. He passed an officer. "Sire, my leg is badly injured and I'm not certain that I can swim."

"So grab a line as you were told," the man snapped.

Moments later Joel reached the deck and was momentarily blinded by the first direct sunlight he had seen in five days. A guard shoved him forward. "Move along!"

Two lines of young slaves were moving across the quarter-deck. As each prisoner reached the starboard rail he climbed up on the rail and leaped overboard. Any prisoner who hesitated in the slightest was immediately seized by a burly sailor and hurled over the rail. Micah was in front of Joel and as he reached the rail he stopped abruptly and called to one of the sailors, "Help him! He's drowning!" He pointed down into the water.

Joel took half a step to one side and looked over the rail. Five yards from the ship, a youth was thrashing frantically and screaming, "Help me! I can't swim!" As Joel watched, the young prisoner's head went under. A moment later he bobbed to the surface, coughing and choking and screaming hysterically, "Help me! Help me!"

Micah was frantic. "He needs help!" he cried, grabbing the sailor's sleeve.

The man struck his hand away. "He's just a slave. No one goes into the water just to save a slave."

"Then I'll help him," Micah replied, stepping up onto the rail.

The sailor grabbed his ankle. "Leave him alone. If you touch him I will kill you when you come back aboard." Micah's mouth fell open as he stared wordlessly at the sailor. The man pushed him and he hit the water with a splash.

The drowning prisoner went under for the last time. Joel saw his grasping hand as it disappeared beneath the waves and he turned away, sickened by what he had just witnessed. Rough hands seized him and in an instant he found himself flying over the rail. He had no time to grab a breath before he hit the water. Cold seawater stung his nose and his eyes and his lungs screamed for air as he clawed for the surface.

His head broke the surface and he gasped for breath and then struck out swimming for the rope ladders hanging over the rail amidships. Just as he reached for the rope ladder it occurred to him—this was the only bath he was going to get. Why not make the most of it? Taking a deep breath, he allowed himself to slide beneath the waves again. He thrashed around in the water for a long moment and then kicked back to the surface. Swimming around for another moment or two to allow as much filth as possible to wash away, at last he swam for the rope ladder and climbed back aboard the ship.

"Move along! Move along!" The guards and sailors were herding the dripping young prisoners back down the stairs to the lower hold. In the stern of the vessel, double lines of young prisoners were following the same procedures. Joel hurried down the stairs and slipped into his usual place at the eighth oar from the front.

Micah looked up at him. "He drowned, Joel. They wouldn't let me help him and he drowned."

Joel nodded. "I saw what happened. There was nothing you could have done about it."

"I could have saved him. He drowned, Joel. I could have saved him!"

"Micah, there was nothing you could do. I heard what the sailor told you."

Micah gritted his teeth. "These people are as cold as snakes. How could anyone be this cruel?"

The guards worked their way back down the rows of slaves, carefully locking leg irons back in place. When a count had been taken and the guards were certain that no one was missing, the cadence drum again began to beat and the rowing commenced. The ship glided forward.

Joel struggled with his emotions as he began to row. He felt intense sorrow at the death of a fellow prisoner. Anger burned in his soul as he thought about the guards who allowed the boy to drown needlessly. And an impending sense of doom overwhelmed him as he thought about his own fate. Where were he and the others being taken? Would he ever return home and see his parents again, or would he die as a slave in some foreign land, far from home and the ones he loved?

He shook his head to clear his thoughts and pulled against the oar with all his might. It felt good to be clean again. It was refreshing to be free from the indescribable filth. He glanced down at his thigh, thankful that the plunge into the salty seawater had cleaned some of the dirt from his wounds. He sighed. *If I could keep the wounds clean, perhaps they would heal properly.*

The cold, dark hold of the slave galley seemed to disappear as the lonely prisoner thought about his home back in Seawell. In his imagination, he was seated at the kitchen table. "I hurt my leg, Ma," he said quietly.

"You hurt your leg," his mother echoed. She set down a pot of greens and turned toward the table. "Let's take a look at it." Caring mother that she was, she actually knelt beside his chair.

Joel pulled back the hem of his tunic, exposing the raw gashes in his thigh, and his mother gasped when she saw them. "Oh, Joel, that looks bad," she said. "How did you do this?"

Joel bit his lip. "A dragon did it."

Ma looked at him, certain that he was teasing, but when she saw his nervous expression she realized that he was not. "Joel, what are you talking about? How would a dragon have done this? Young man, sometimes you do go on so."

"I—I was fighting him," Joel confessed.

Joel's mother stood to her feet, immersed a small cloth in a bucket of fresh spring water, and then knelt and began to scrub at the wounds. "Arg!" Joel groaned, trying hard to keep from screaming. "Ma, that's hurts!"

"Son, we can't let this get infected," Ma replied, continuing to scrub away at the injury. "If we don't get this cleaned out, it will." She bit her lip as she worked, for she realized that she was hurting him. "Now, how did you say this happened?"

"I was fighting a dragon."

"Fighting a dragon. All right. And just how—" His words suddenly registered and she stopped, stunned. She stared at him for several long seconds and then said in a voice barely above a whisper, "Son, please tell me that you are jesting."

He shook his head. "I got these injuries fighting a dragon."

She studied his face for several long moments and decided that he was telling the truth. "Son, what would cause you to do a thing like that? You could have been killed!"

"He trapped me beneath a ledge and raked my thigh with his claws," Joel replied, suddenly feeling extremely foolish as he attempted to explain the incident. "Since I was under the ledge he couldn't get at me to kill me but I couldn't get away or fight him effectively, either."

Ma put her hand to her head. "Oh, Joel. Son, when will you ever learn?" Shaking her head in disbelief, she continued to scrub at the wound.

Joel had always hated it when his mother used that expression, but just now he realized that she used it out of her concern for him. As frustrated as she was with him, he now could see that she was deeply worried about him. He watched her as she opened a tiny vial and poured a trickle of amber fluid into the gashes. She tore a strip of cloth from a garment to make a bandage and he saw with dismay that it was her spare blouse, the only one she had other than the one she was wearing.

"So again, tell me how and why you were fighting a dragon." She looked up at him and he saw a tenderness in her eyes that he had never before noticed. "You're telling me that you got these wounds by fighting a real, live dragon."

Joel nodded. "I was at the Dragon Tournament on the Isle of Dragons. Lank tricked me into going into the arena and fighting a dragon. The dragon pinned Lank, and I rescued him and saved his life, but when the dragon got the best of me Lank turned and ran for his life. I thought he was my friend, but. . . ."

"Joel, Joel. After what happened with the money from the *Princess* I would think you would keep your distance from that ruffian. Son, he's not your friend."

"I know that now," Joel replied ruefully.

Ma began to wrap the bandage around his leg. "'He that walketh with wise men shall be wise, but a companion of fools shall be destroyed.' Joel, you could have very easily have been killed." Pulling the bandage tight, she tore the end into separate strips and then deftly knotted them to hold the binding in place. She looked up at him and he felt as if she could see right into the depths of his soul. "Does your father know about this?"

Joel shook his head miserably. "I—I'd rather that he didn't find out. I—I don't want to lose his trust in me."

"It's a little late for that now, don't you think?" She ran her hand over her handiwork. "You're going to have quite a limp for awhile. Do you really think that your father is not going to notice?"

He shook his head again.

"Did you say this was on the Isle of Dragons?"

He nodded.

"Last night?"

"Aye."

Ma sighed deeply and sat silent on the floor beside him for several long moments. Joel waited nervously. "So tell me what made you go into an arena with a live dragon. Son, don't you realize how dangerous that was? Don't you realize how utterly foolish that was?"

He nodded again. "I do now."

"So why did you do it? Why would you go face to face with a dragon, knowing that it could kill you? What were you thinking?" Her face showed her disappointment and he knew that she was not scolding him out of frustration, but rather, out of a deep sense of concern for his wellbeing.

"Lank—Lank talked me into it."

"You did it because Lank wanted you to? Joel, we both know that Lank is not a friend of yours, nor a friend of this family. Why in Terrestria would you do something this dangerous just to please a...a do nothing that tried to rob you of the money that was to pay off your father's ship? Son, that doesn't even make sense!"

He sighed heavily. "I know that now."

"So why did you do it?"

He sighed again. "I guess maybe I did it to make friends."

"To make friends? Friends like Lank?"

"Ma, I've always felt like an outcast among the youth of this town. I don't really have any friends. I don't fit in. When Lank started being friendly to me and invited me to the Dragon Tournament, I thought it would be a way to make some friends."

Her expression softened and he knew that she was listening. Her eyes glistened and he saw tears.

"I started going to the Tournaments every Friday night. I've been going for over three months."

She frowned. "Three months?"

Joel nodded. "Aye. I knew it was wrong and I knew it was dangerous and I knew that you and Pa would be disappointed if you found out, but...well, once I started going I couldn't seem to stop. The Tournaments were exciting, and there were lots of young people there, and. . . ." He fell silent.

"And then Lank asked you to actually participate and you couldn't refuse him."

He nodded miserably. "I wanted to be part of his group and I wanted the other fellows to like me, and... and then there was Myra."

"Myra? Who's Myra?"

As Joel started to tell about Myra, his mother's face began to pale and the kitchen grew dark. He reached out to her, grabbing her arm, but she was pulled from his grasp by an unseen force. She faded from view, seemingly getting farther and farther away from him. "Wait, Ma!" he cried out. "Come back! Ma, don't leave me!"

The room was dark and smelled of salt and unwashed bodies. He moved his foot and heard the dull clank of a heavy chain. Looking around, he realized that he was still in the gloomy hold of the slave galley. His heart ached as he realized that he had been dreaming. *If only I had known,* he lamented. *If only I had realized just how much Ma and Pa loved me. If only I could see them one more time.*

Bitter tears flowed freely in the darkness.

Chapter Ten

Wynn and Cobby stood at the top of the stairs, silently gazing down into the empty, sun-splashed arena. Cobby took a deep, trembling breath as he scanned the vast amphitheater, taking in the terraced seats now littered with empty steins, puddles of spilled ale and rum, and torn articles of clothing. He sniffed the air. Glancing down again at the sandy floor of the arena, he cringed as images from the past paraded across the vista of his memory.

A raging dragon charged across the sand, bellowing in fury, and Cobby actually covered both ears with his hands as if he could somehow shut out the sound. The great beast abruptly stopped in its tracks, silently scanning the arena. Cobby trembled as the dragon started toward him. He could see the huge claws digging into the sand with every step, hear the snorting, rasping of its breathing, smell the putrid stench of death and decay as it lumbered closer and closer. . . .

"Come on, Son." Wynn's voice shattered the moment and the terrifying images vanished instantly. The amphitheater was silent and empty.

Cobby nervously licked his lips. "This place hasn't changed."

Wynn nodded wordlessly, knowing what his son was experiencing. The memories of the past were very real and very painful.

"If only I had warned him, Pa." Cobby lifted a trembling hand to his mouth and bit the back of his knuckles as his eyes slowly filled with tears. "If only I had warned him about this place."

"You won't accomplish anything by blaming yourself, Cobby. And Joel did make his own choice."

Cobby nodded miserably. "But I could have warned him! I could have told him about this wretched, cursed place, but I had no idea that he would ever be tempted to come here." He looked up at his father and the tears streamed down his face. "When the townspeople talked about the youth of Seawell attending the Dragon Tournaments again, I never dreamed that Joel would be involved! How could I have been so blind? How could I have not seen the signs?"

Wynn sighed deeply. "We all missed them, Cobby."

"But it should have been so clear! For the last two or three months he's been so tired every Saturday morning—that should have been a dead giveaway! I should have realized that he was out late on Friday nights."

"We all missed it, Cobby."

"I'm his father, Pa. The responsibility is mine."

Wynn shrugged. "His Majesty's book places a heavy responsibility on the grandparents too, Son. I'm as much to blame as you."

Cobby took a deep breath and turned toward the arena. "Will you go down there with me?"

"Of course."

With heavy hearts, the two men slowly descended the stairs. Cobby trembled as they reached the bottom, and Wynn put a hand on his shoulder, squeezing firmly. "This place stills smells of death and decay, Pa."

Cobby slid back one of the heavy panels and stepped out onto the sand. He turned, and for an instant, the stands were filled to capacity with cheering, frolicking youth, all wildly screaming his name. His hand was filled with a cold, hard object and he realized that he was gripping a sword. He whirled and the dragon was upon him. "No!" he screamed, and his voice echoed across the vast emptiness of the amphitheater.

"Cobby! Let it go, Son."

The dragon vanished. Cobby turned in time to see the crowd fade from view. His hand was empty.

Cobby nodded. "I'm all right, Pa."

The tears streamed down his face as he strode briskly across the arena. There was no missing the myriad tracks in the sand—human footprints in abundance, but also, the splayed, three-toed tracks of enormous, bloodthirsty monsters. The tracks in the sand told a story, and he had enough experience in the arena to read the tale.

He paused at the far side of the arena. The sand was stained with blood and deeply marked with the signs of a struggle. He knelt and peered beneath a projecting ledge of sandstone. More blood. He reached in, and with trembling fingers plucked a fragment of blood-stained cloth from the sand. He gasped as he brought it into the light.

Wynn was at his elbow. "What is it? What's wrong?"

Cobby trembled violently. For a long moment he couldn't speak. "Pa—" He took a deep breath and tried again. "Pa, what if this is Joel's?"

"Joel's tunic was green, Cobby, not red and yellow."

Cobby nodded wordlessly and allowed the scrap to fall from his fingers. He stood and scanned the arena and then the vast seating area. "Let's get out of here."

Wynn gripped his arm. "Let's go down to the boats, Son. Perchance Saul and the others have found something."

The two retraced their steps and soon were making their way down a narrow set of stairs that hugged the face of the cliff. Cobby glanced down at the secluded cove. The *Princess* bobbed gently in the swells, nudging repeatedly against the dock like a persistent child seeking attention from its mother. As Wynn and Cobby reached the bottom of the stairs, five men strode across the sand to meet them.

Cobby greeted them anxiously with a single word: "Anything?"

Saul, the tall reeve of Seawell, soberly shook his head. "I'm sorry, Cobby. There's not much to go on. There's plenty of evidence that the Tournament was held last night and there are signs that the young ones were taken as slaves, but beyond that—"

"What signs?" Wynn interrupted. "What signs that they were taken as slaves?"

Saul hesitated.

"Tell us," Wynn demanded. "It won't help to hide anything from us."

Saul nodded. "There are plenty of tracks going from the stairs here to the dock. Tracks of young people walking single file and larger tracks of soldiers—we can tell by their boots. That can only mean one thing, Wynn. And not only that, but there are other marks in the sand, imprints of chains." He hesitated again. "And there's blood."

Some of the men began to weep, Cobby among them.

"You're sure it's the youth of Seawell?"

The reeve nodded. "Some of their siblings knew about the Tournament but didn't say anything to their parents until this morning. We've heard from several of them this morning; that's how we knew to come here."

One of the men spoke up. "We found Lank's body. We believe he's the one responsible for much of this."

"But there were more than just the youth of Seawell involved," Cobby argued. "From the looks of the litter in the amphitheater, there must have been thousands of young ones here last night!"

Saul nodded again. "Apparently this was the big Tournament. They drew the youth from cities and towns from quite a few miles around. Once they brought them here and got them drunk enough, they took them captive."

The seven men walked slowly across the beach toward the waiting cog. "Is there any way to tell where they were taken?" Cobby asked, doing his best to keep his emotions in check.

The reeve stopped and looked deeply into his eyes. "I wish there was, Cobby, but they could have been taken to any of a dozen places. The Karnivans are known to be heavily involved in the slave trade, but so are the Nidians and the Ooslotts. And of course, there's always Corthia and Araban and Carifa—all three are active centers of the slave trade." He shook his head. "I'm sorry, men, but there's no way of knowing where these young ones were taken."

"We can't just give up on them!" Cobby blurted.

"What are you going to do, Cobby, search all of Terrestria for Joel? A man could spend his entire life and never find him. Karniva and Nidia and Carifa are vast countries—you could never search them in a hundred years. Araban by itself has more than three hundred thousand people. Corthia is said to have over a million. I'm sorry to say this, Cobby, but there's simply no way to find Joel or any of the others."

"We can try," Cobby replied fiercely. "Saul, we're talking about my son! I'd give my life to bring him back."

Saul nodded. "I know you would, Cobby." He stooped and picked up a stone. Drawing back his arm, he hurled the stone as far as he could across the surging waters of the cove. "My friend, can you bring back that stone?"

"That would be impossible..." Cobby began, and then started to sob.

"Gentlemen," Saul said quietly, and his lip quivered as he spoke, "the only thing I can tell you is to commit your sons and daughters to the keeping of King Emmanuel. He alone knows where your children have been taken."

Wynn slipped close to Cobby and put an arm around his shoulders.

"Let's head for the *Princess*," Saul said hoarsely. "Gentlemen, I'm sorry."

The somber group walked slowly across the sand. Cobby and Wynn clutched each other as if one would collapse without the other. Seagulls swarmed overhead, soaring and screeching. The sun was dropping quickly toward the horizon.

Cobby's eyes were blurred with tears but his attention was arrested by a sparkle of blue light in the sand. He stooped and picked up a translucent blue stone that gleamed in the sunlight.

"What is it, Cobby?"

The fisherman shrugged. "Just a trifle," he replied wearily. "Just a pretty blue pebble, I'm afraid." He displayed the stone for the others to see and then drew back his arm, intending to hurl it into the waves.

Saul seized his arm. "Wait, Cobby. Let me see it."

Puzzled, Cobby handed the blue stone to the reeve.

Saul studied the unusual stone for a long moment. "Unless I'm mistaken," he said slowly, "this is Corthian lapis."

"It's what?"

"Corthian lapis," Saul repeated. "It's a semiprecious stone found nowhere in Terrestria except near Corthia. The Corthians prize it highly and use it to adorn their clothing and jewelry. Their soldiers use it to decorate their shields and the hilts of their swords, believing that it gives them favor with their deities when they go into battle."

Cobby's heart leaped. "This is the clue for which we've been searching!" he shouted. "Our children were taken to Corthia!"

Saul sadly shook his head. "We don't know that, Cobby. Don't get your hopes up."

"I will go to Corthia!" Cobby exclaimed. "I will find my son!"

The reeve gripped him by the shoulders. "Cobby, Cobby, please hear me, my friend. Even if Joel was taken to Corthia, you would never find him. Corthia has more than a million people! It would be like searching the bay for the pebble I just tossed in. Your chances of finding him are nil."

"He's my son," Cobby insisted. "I will go to Corthia and bring him back home."

One of the other men spoke up. "Saul's right, Cobby. You could spend a lifetime in Corthia and never find him."

"Then I will spend a lifetime, if necessary," Cobby replied. "I failed my son once; I will not fail him again. I will bring Joel home again or give my life trying." He turned toward the *Princess*. "Let's go home, my friends. There is much that I must do in preparation for my journey."

Chapter Eleven

"Corthia off the port bow!" The lookout's voice rang throughout the ship, bringing cheers from the sailors and soldiers.

Joel's heart pounded as the slave galley glided into a harbor. He could see just enough through the oar port to tell that the harbor was immense, with wide waterways and tall docks to accommodate large ships. The cadence drum abruptly ceased its steady pounding and the prisoners rested on their oars, thankful for some relief. Joel turned to Micah. "So tell me more about Corthia," he requested.

His companion shrugged. "That's not much to tell," he replied. "Corthia is a city-state, meaning that it has its own government and is ruled by no king."

"Everyone is ruled by King Emmanuel," Joel replied, "whether they recognize it or not."

"Not the Corthians," Micah insisted. "They refuse to acknowledge his authority over their city. They have an independent government with a governor, a parliament, and a senate." He shifted on the narrow bench in an attempt to find a comfortable position. "The Corthians are known throughout Terrestria as men of the sea; in fact, they have established trade routes to almost every corner of the kingdom. Their armies and their navies have conquered all of the surrounding regions and they levy heavy tributes from their neighbors. It's one of the wealthiest cities anywhere. Wait until we get off the ship—you won't believe your eyes."

"What's going to happen to us?" Jared inquired, and Joel waited tensely, for he had been wrestling with the same question.

"We're slaves," Micah answered simply, "or at least we will be as soon as they sell us at auction." He chuckled, but there was no humor in his voice. "Unless, of course, we end up as sacrifices in the temples."

"Do you think we might?" Jared's eyes revealed his anxiety.

Micah shook his head. "I doubt it. All three of us are strong and healthy. They usually offer the weakest or the sickly as sacrifices; they never give their deities their best." He glanced at Joel. "Of course, one might end up as a sacrifice if one had something drastically wrong with him—say a serious leg injury or something like that."

Joel grinned and shook his head. "Thanks, friend."

The guards passed through the hold, using their keys to free the prisoners from the cluster chains but leaving the heavy leg irons in place. Chains clanked as row after row of prisoners were led up the stairs to the upper deck. When Joel reached the deck he stood blinking against the brightness of the sun. A guard cuffed him on the shoulder. "Keep moving!"

Shading his eyes against the noonday sun, Joel stepped forward. Another guard thumped him on the chest with a huge fist. "Hold up, knave! You're not going anywhere." The man knelt and passed a heavy cluster chain through Joel's shackles, securing him in a line with eleven other prisoners. He slapped Joel on the back of his injured thigh and a spasm of pain shot through Joel's body. "Move along now."

Trembling with anticipation, Joel followed the line of

prisoners across the deck and down the gangway to stand upon a wide, busy wharf. Tall ships flying a variety of flags lined the wharves. Sailors strolled the docks, laughing and cursing with their comrades while longshoremen unloaded the ships and wheeled heavy loads to various destinations.

Joel and his companions stared. Before them stretched wide, wide boulevards of gray cobblestones flanked on either side by imposing buildings of glistening marble. The streets were crowded with luxurious carriages pulled by elegant horses whose harnesses were adorned with gold and silver and shining blue stones. The residents of the city were dressed in rich silks, satins and costly brocades, and displayed inordinate amounts of jewels and gold. As far as the eye could see, magnificent buildings rose to form a skyline that was certainly impressive, if not intimidating. Corthia was a city of wealth and splendor.

"Did you ever see such a place?" one young prisoner breathed, his eyes wide with amazement. "This must be the most magnificent city in all Terrestria!"

Joel stared at the majestic city, unimpressed by the grandeur before him. He longed for home, and to him the city of Corthia was nothing more than a magnificent prison. Soldiers were everywhere, strolling the streets and wharves, standing in doorways and alleys, watching, watching, watching. Their shields bore images of the Corthian war bird with eyes formed by two shining blue stones. The same blue stones adorned the hilts of their swords. Joel shuddered. There was an atmosphere of oppression, of tyranny, of cruelty. *Will I ever again see Seawell?*

"Move along now," a heavyset guard ordered, slapping the lead slave on the back of the head and then laughing at his pain. "I have to get you lads sold so that I get home in time for supper." Chains clanked as the line of slaves moved forward.

Moments later the wharf was filled with fearful young slaves as the other ships unloaded their human cargoes.

As the guard marched them through the busy streets of Corthia, Joel was surprised that no one paid them the slightest attention. Apparently, the residents were accustomed to seeing large numbers of slaves.

After a ten-minute walk the group of slaves approached a tall, imposing building with massive white pillars and a wide portico of polished black marble. "You had better hope you don't get bought by Lord Tarak," the guard told them cheerfully. "I understand that he's bidding today."

"Who is Lord Tarak?" one lad ventured to ask.

The guard gave him an amused glance. "Lord Tarak is one of the wealthiest men in Corthia," he replied, "but also one of the cruelest. His overseers take delight in inflicting pain upon his slaves. If you are purchased by one of his stewards, you won't live to see your next birthday." He laughed. "Or at least you won't want to."

Joel's heart constricted with fear as he stared at the man. *Is all of Corthia this hardened? How can this man speak of such cruelty and then laugh about it?*

The guard led them around behind the building to a huge, open courtyard. At one side was a large, raised platform; on either side of that, two large fenced-off areas for the slaves. As Joel passed through the gate into the holding area the man noticed his limp. He sidled over next to Joel. "Tall boy," he said in a low voice, "don't limp when you walk across the auction block."

Joel was confused. "Sir?"

"If you limp across the auction block, I'll kill you," the man growled. "I want you to bring as high a price as possible."

Joel nodded wordlessly. He crowded into the enclosure with

scores of other young male slaves as the females were filing into the enclosure on the opposite end of the platform. His heart pounded. *Please don't let me be sold to Lord Tarak,* he implored silently. *Anyone but Lord Tarak.*

His nervousness increased as the enclosure grew more and more crowded. The prisoners were pushing and jostling and he found himself shoved against a young servant who was keeping the gate. Moving over to make room, he stepped on the lad's foot and was startled by a howl of pain. "I'm sorry!" Joel blurted, moving quickly to one side.

The lad was hopping on one foot. "I'm sorry," Joel said again. "Are you all right?"

To Joel's relief, the lad gave him a wide grin. "I'll live," he replied. "Just try not to do it again, huh?"

Joel nodded and gave him an apologetic smile. "I'll try not to."

"My name is Zachary," the boy said. "I'm in charge of the gate for the auction. You sure are tall! Where are you from?"

"I'm Joel and I'm from Seawell," Joel replied, taken aback at the lad's friendliness. "I'm told it's more than a thousand miles from here. Right now I'd give anything to be back there."

The boy nodded. "I'm sorry you have to be sold," he said with a sympathetic wag of the head. "I just hope you don't get sold to Lord Tarak. He's a mean one."

"I've heard that," Joel replied with a grimace. "Is he here today?"

"His steward is," Zachary told him. "See that fat man on the front row of buyers? The one with the bright turban? That's Vardaman. If he starts bidding on you, you know you're in trouble!" With these words, Zachary climbed up on the gate and turned his attention to the business at hand.

Oh, that I had never heard of the Dragon Tournament, Joel thought miserably. *If only I had never listened to Lank. If only I had been wise enough to realize that he was not a friend!*

His melancholy thoughts turned to home. *I wonder what Pa is doing right now. I wonder what he thought when he learned that I was at the Tournament. I wonder what he thinks of me now. If I could somehow walk through the front door, would Pa take me back?*

His eyes welled with tears as he thought about his mother. *What did it do to Ma when she learned that I was missing? She doesn't even know where I am. She doesn't even know if I'm alive or dead! I'm sorry, Ma.*

Guards passed among the prisoners. "Tunics down!" they shouted. "Bare your backs!"

Joel turned. "What?"

"Bare your back!" A guard grabbed him, ripping the front of his tunic open and pulling it down around his waist to bare his chest and back, arms and shoulders. The man spotted the bloody bandage on his thigh. "What's that?"

"I was injured, sir."

The guard responded by pulling his tunic lower so that the hem concealed the bandage.

Joel glanced across to the other enclosure and was embarrassed to see that the female slaves were being treated in the same fashion and exposed in the same way. He thought of Myra. *I wonder what happened to her. I wonder if she's still alive.*

A tall man in elegant clothing strode onto the platform and walked to the center. He flashed a wide, toothy smile to the crowd of buyers as he raised his voice. "Gentlemen, we won't keep you waiting a moment longer. We know that you're here to purchase the finest that Corthia has to offer, and today you won't be disappointed! Have we got some fine specimens for you!" The auctioneer then made a couple of crude remarks about the female slaves, which drew laughter from the crowd.

"Gentlemen, we want to move rapidly and I ask that you

respond quickly. As soon as you know you have the winning bid, move forward to pay the cashier and claim your purchase. We have a lot of quality merchandise today and we don't want to waste any of your valuable time."

He turned to two assistants. "Bring out the first three males." Zachary opened the gate and an assistant selected three of the youth closest to the gate. As Joel watched in stunned silence, the auctioneer launched into fast-paced chatter as he attempted to get the highest possible price for his human merchandise. Talking so fast that Joel could scarcely understand him, he quickly sold all three lads to the highest bidders. He then asked for three females and sold them in the same fashion.

Zachary opened the gate again and Joel found himself thrust out upon the platform with two other hapless lads. He did his best to walk without limping, though the pain was almost unbearable. His heart began to pound. His chest constricted and he struggled to breathe. Standing before the crowd of eager buyers, he found that he was terrified. He watched Lord Tarak's steward, Vardaman. The man scanned the other two young slaves with disdain and then glanced at Joel. To Joel's dismay, he looked Joel up and down with interest.

"We'll start with the slave on my left," the auctioneer called. "What am I bid for this fine young man? Strong, healthy, and good for years and years of work. Do I hear two hundred?"

"One hundred karvas."

The auctioneer raised both hands. "This fine young man is easily worth twice that! Do I hear one-fifty?"

Joel glanced at the youth and saw the fear written in his eyes.

"One-fifty," a man called.

"I have one-fifty, but do I hear one-eighty? One hundred

eighty karvas for a healthy young slave that is easily worth more than two hundred."

Moments later the winning bid was one hundred seventy and the youth was sold. Joel sympathized with the young slave as he was led away.

"Next we have a tall, young man with hair like fire," the auctioneer said with a wide grin. "Who'll start the bidding on this fine slave?"

Joel was horrified as Lord Tarak's steward raised one hand. "One hundred."

"I have a hundred, but this lad is easily worthy three times that," the auctioneer called. "Gentlemen, let's do this young man justice! Do I hear two-fifty?"

"Two hundred," a man on the end called.

"Two-twenty." Vardaman had raised his bid. Joel held his breath.

"Two-forty."

"Two-fifty."

The biding continued until the price had reached three hundred karvas. Vardaman seemed displeased that the bidding had gone that high and turned away in disgust. The man on the end made one more bid. "Three hundred ten."

Joel's heart leaped. Apparently, Lord Tarak's steward was out of the bidding. He knew nothing about the man who had just made the bid, but at least he could not be as bad as Lord Tarak.

Vardaman turned back, raising his hand halfway as he thought it through.

Joel held his breath.

The fat steward lowered his hand. The look on his face said that he had decided against making another bid.

Joel was relieved.

"I have a bid for three hundred and ten karvas," the

auctioneer called. "Do I hear three hundred twenty? Three hundred ten…"

"Three twenty." To Joel's chagrin, Vardaman had raised his hand and made another bid.

"I have three twenty for the tall slave with the fiery hair," the auctioneer called. "Do I hear another bid? Three thirty? Three forty?"

Joel watched the other bidder hopefully, but the man didn't move. Joel's heart pounded fiercely.

"Three twenty… three twenty… sold for three hundred twenty karvas!"

Joel felt sick as the fat steward made his way to the stairs to claim his purchase. *I'm going to belong to Lord Tarak! This is the worst thing that could have happened! The very nobleman that we were warned about has bought me.* Fear washed over him and he felt as if he would collapse.

Vardaman reached out and grasped Joel's upper arm as if to check his strength. Joel responded by tensing his arm to tighten the muscles. Suddenly the man tightened his grip, squeezing Joel's arm so fiercely that it seemed his fingers would penetrate the boy's flesh. Joel winced and tried to jerk his arm away but Vardaman maintained his grip and continued to squeeze until Joel thought that he would pass out from the intense pain. Looking directly into Joel's eyes, the man smiled, but his eyes were cold and cruel. "Pull up your tunic and follow me," he said, abruptly releasing Joel's arm. "Don't just stand there like a stick."

He turned to an assistant who hovered nearby. "Keep him with you."

As Vardaman moved away through the crowd, the other man motioned to Joel. "Come with me."

Pulling his tunic back into place, Joel turned to follow the second man. Vardaman was at his side in a flash, grabbing him in a headlock and twisting until Joel was sure that his neck was about to break. "I told you to follow me," he growled. "Slave, you had better learn to listen and follow directions."

"Aye, sir," Joel grunted weakly. "I will, sir."

Vardaman released him. "What are you going to do, slave?"

Joel rubbed his neck. "Follow you, sir."

"You learn quickly, slave. That's good. Remember what you've just learned and you'll live." He looked at his assistant. "Take him away."

Vardaman hurried back to his place on the front line of the buyers, but Joel hesitated for a moment or two before he turned to follow the assistant. "Stand here," the man told him as they reached the back of the crowd.

It was no exaggeration to say that Lord Tarak's men are cruel, Joel thought as he watched the auction continue. *If Vardaman's treatment of me is any indication of what is to come, I may not live to see my next birthday.*

Fear gripped his heart and a cold premonition settled upon him like a heavy weight. Alone and helpless in a hostile city, he suddenly felt very small and vulnerable.

Chapter Twelve

Chained together like animals, the lines of dejected slaves trudged wearily up the steep lane. They shuffled listlessly, heads down, their eyes blank and staring, their shoulders slumped forlornly as if they had long ago given up all hope. The last slave in a line of twenty, Joel plodded along with the others. Like the hapless souls around him, his candle of hope had been snuffed out.

His feet were blistered and bleeding and his injured leg now throbbed continuously. The heavy shackles around his ankles had rubbed the flesh raw. Every step was torture. Having eaten nothing that day or the day previous, his stomach was empty and his energy was gone. So weary that he was not even conscious of what he was doing, he simply trudged along, mechanically putting one foot in front of the other.

His physical suffering was minor when compared to the agony within his soul. He now knew that he would never again see his parents or his grandfather, and the realization brought with it a pain that he would not long survive. The fire within his soul had been extinguished and it would simply be a matter of time before he yielded to the temptation to lie down and die. Life as a slave was simply not worth living.

The slave in front of him stumbled and fell and did not get up again, bringing the entire line to a halt. Joel was still lucid enough to realize what was happening and to anticipate the terrible beating that Vardaman would inflict upon the youth if he delayed the journey. Bending over, he gasped the lad under the arms and attempted to lift him to his feet, but the form in his arms was as limp as a rag doll. "Get up," he urged in a fierce whisper. "Get up or they'll beat you!"

Suddenly a steely hand gripped the collar of Joel's tunic, twisting it until the garment tightened around his throat, choking him. A harsh voice exploded in his ear. "What are you doing?" Vardaman screamed.

Releasing the helpless youth, Joel stood upright. "I—I was t-trying to help this fellow," he stammered.

"Did I order you to help?" Vardaman demanded, leaning in so that his face was mere inches from Joel's. "Is this lad your responsibility?"

"Nay, sir," Joel replied nervously.

"Then don't touch him!" the steward screamed, striking Joel across the face with the wooden handle of his whip.

The smoldering embers on the hearth of Joel's soul suddenly burst into flame. Without thinking about the consequences of his actions, he came to the defense of his comrade. "He hasn't eaten yesterday or today," Joel retorted. "How long do you expect him to go without food?"

Vardaman was enraged. "No slave talks to me that way," he snarled, striking Joel in the face again. "When we stop for rest tonight, you'll sleep standing up. You'll also receive no food or water until we reach Lord Tarak's estate. Slave boy, you'll learn not to tread in where you're not invited."

Joel knew better than to reply.

Vardaman turned to an overseer and gestured toward the

inert figure on the ground. "Unchain him and throw him on one of the wagons," he ordered. "Lash him to the load so he doesn't fall off."

"Aye, sir."

Half an hour later the caravan stopped for the night in a park-like area beside a quiet stream. Guards were posted around the perimeter and then the slaves were allowed to collapse in the grass. Two timid servants brought gourds of water from the stream, followed by earthenware bowls of thin gruel.

True to his word, Vardaman had Joel chained to a tree in a standing position and gave strict instructions that he was to receive no food or water. The exhausted young slave knew that no one would dare to defy the cruel steward's order.

Other groups of slaves, male and female, made their way into the park. As one large group passed the tree where he was shackled, Joel saw a familiar face. His heart leaped and he called out before he could restrain himself. "Myra!"

The girl glanced over her shoulder and her eyes widened when she saw him. Before she could respond she was dragged away with the group. *She's still alive,* Joel thought gratefully. *I may never see her again, but at least I know that she's alive.*

An hour later the park was quiet as the countless groups of slaves settled in for the night. Sagging against the chains that bound him to the tree, Joel did his best to get comfortable enough to sleep. The chains were just long enough to prevent him from sitting down, and after a few minutes of experimentation he discovered that this had been deliberately planned to create the greatest amount of discomfort possible. The chains were fastened low enough so that he couldn't support himself against them while standing, yet couldn't sit down, either.

This is going to be a long, long night, he thought dejectedly.

Thoroughly exhausted, he finally leaned his back against the tree and attempted to sleep standing up.

Late in the afternoon of the next day, the caravan made its way up a steep slope and then traveled across a narrow bridge suspended over a deep canyon. The feet of the weary slaves made a rhythmic staccato on the planks of the structure and the bridge swayed from side to side under their weight.

Intrigued by the unusual structure, Joel leaned out over the side cable and looked down as he crossed. The gorge was barely fifty feet across, but he estimated that it was nearly three hundred feet deep. Rugged vertical walls of red sandstone fell away to a meandering creek far below. Glancing back to be sure that he was not being observed, he snatched a pebble from the roadway and tossed it over the side, then watched as it fell down, down, down to the water below.

He shuddered. *If someone fell over the side, it would take forever for him to hit the bottom!* Just a bit unnerved, he moved away from the side. He felt a sense of relief when his feet were on solid ground once again.

Fifteen minutes later the caravan halted before a massive gateway of glistening brass, the only visible entrance through the high stone wall surrounding a vast estate. "Welcome to Chamac, the home of Lord Tarak," Vardaman called in a voice that the entire convoy could hear. "I will remind you that you are now the property of Lord Tarak and that from now on you exist only for his pleasure. Your life is his, and should he decide that you are no longer profitable to him, he can choose to end it at any time. You will obey my orders and those of my overseers, for we speak for Lord Tarak.

"The shackles around your ankles are permanent, for you

belong to Lord Tarak and we must be certain that his property does not get lost." He grinned at them. "One thing you should know: Lord Tarak has twelve of the most vicious boar hounds in all Corthia. You need not fear them, for they are kept in a kennel during the day. But hear this—they are released each night to run free within the grounds. Should any slave be foolhardy enough to attempt an escape, these dogs will find you and tear you to shreds. Believe me; they would love to have the opportunity."

He glanced across the crowd of anxious young slaves. "As I said, welcome to Chamac. I am Vardaman, steward of Lord Tarak's estate. As his property, you will answer to me and to my overseers." He scanned the faces of his captive audience, and when he came to Joel his gaze lingered for a long moment. "My job is to make you wish you had never been born. And believe me, I love my job. Before long, you will learn to hate me almost as much as I hate you."

He grinned again. "Let me show you what I am talking about." He scanned the group before him and his gaze fell upon a slender young girl. He pointed her out with the handle of his whip. "You. Step forward."

An overseer hurried over and freed the girl from the chain, allowing her to move away from the group. "What is your name?" Vardaman demanded.

"M-Marah, sir." The girl was trembling.

"Marah. Well, Marah, I don't like the way you look. I think I'll make some changes." Suddenly the whip in his hand lashed out, striking the terrified girl across the face and cutting a large gash in her cheek. With a scream of terror the girl threw her hands to her face. A trickle of blood flowed down her wrist.

Vardaman laughed. "Thank you, Marah. Return to your place in line." Sobbing, the terrified girl shuffled back to join the others.

The evil man stalked slowly toward the stunned group of slaves, who cowered as he approached. "You're afraid of me," he sneered. "That's good. You're thinking that I had no reason to strike Marah, and you're right. I did it simply because I wanted to. Never forget that I can do anything I want to you. Anything. At any time." He whirled and kicked one of the slaves in the stomach. The youth bent over, clutching his stomach and gasping for breath. The rest of the group recoiled in horror. Vardaman laughed.

Slowly, and with great finesse, the steward coiled his whip. "Welcome to Chamac. In the ancient languages the name means 'cruelty' and you will soon learn that Lord Tarak's estate lives up to its name."

The entourage of slaves passed through the gates and entered a vast, elegant estate. Well-manicured lawns and exquisite flower gardens stretched as far as the eye could see. Fountains and statuary and groves of well-kept fruit trees added to the grandeur of the property. Nearly a mile in the distance, on a promontory overlooking the estate, perched a magnificent castle with soaring towers and turrets. Three or four furlongs to the east of the castle stood an enormous, half-finished edifice of gleaming marble.

Joel was trembling with rage at the cruelties he had just witnessed. *Someday,* he vowed, *I will kill this snake! I don't know when or how, but I will do it.*

He looked up to realize that Vardaman was looking directly at him, and the sneering grin made Joel wonder if the man could somehow read his thoughts. Deep in his soul he knew that trouble lay ahead.

After a meager supper of boiled greens and cornmeal mush, the new slaves spent their first night at Chamac outdoors, chained together in a fenced-in enclosure under a grove of pecan trees. Joel tossed and turned, trying to find a comfortable sleeping position, but the ground was hard and unyielding. Exhausted as he was, he still found that sleep eluded him. Every little noise of the night seemed to be amplified a thousand times and his mind refused to rest. His aching body craved sleep, but his imagination was lively and the possibilities it conjured up were terrifying.

He heard a snuffling, snorting sound and looked over to see the dark silhouette of a large dog sniffing along the edge of the fence. The dog was enormous, the biggest Joel had ever seen, with a large head and heavy jowls. *A Karnivan boar hound,* Joel surmised. *I'm sure glad that there's a fence between us. That thing looks vicious!* As Joel watched in fascinated horror, the huge dog clawed at the fence as if anxious to get at the slaves inside. With an ominous growl rumbling in the depths of its chest, the dog began to bite the fence itself.

That thing could kill a man, Joel thought with a shudder. *One thing's for sure—no slave will ever escape at night.* The boar hound continued to chew and claw relentlessly at the iron fence for nearly an hour before it wandered away into the darkness.

Joel was in the depths of despair. *There is no way to escape from this wretched place. Shackled and guarded by overseers by day and chained together at night, guarded by dogs that would eat us alive— there is no way anyone could escape.* Finally, just two hours before dawn, Joel drifted into a restless, dreamless slumber.

He was awakened by a sharp kick in the ribs. His eyes flew open and he found himself staring up into the stern face of an overseer. "Get up and get moving!" the man growled. He drew back his boot for a second kick. Joel saw it coming and rolled to his feet, though his aching muscles protested at the sudden call to action.

Joel stretched and looked around. The estate was still dark, with a gray light stealing across the fields. Sunrise was at least half an hour away.

"Here." Another overseer thrust a cold bowl of gruel into his hands. "Eat this and be quick about it. Your work detail starts in just a few minutes."

Joel had barely finished gulping the tasteless substance when Vardaman appeared, his pudgy hands caressing the whip as if it were his most prized possession. His eyes narrowed when he saw Joel. "Have I got a work assignment for you, tall boy," he gloated. "We'll soon see just how tough you really are."

Moments later Joel found himself assigned to a heavy construction detail. An enormous building was taking shape on the east side of the estate and Joel joined hundreds of other slaves in hauling the materials for the structure.

He spent the first part of the morning helping a work crew of slaves move a massive block of marble to the building site. Six feet tall, three feet wide and twelve feet long, the stone weighed many tons and was moved along on a series of wooden rollers placed beneath it. Several slaves behind the block pushed against it while scores of others pulled long ropes fastened around it. As each roller was freed behind the marble block, a slave grabbed it and dashed forward to place it in front of the block again.

Progress was slow but all went well until the workers took the heavy block up an inclined ramp. The block was rolling steadily along, slowly inching its way upward, when a rope suddenly broke with a loud report like a crack of thunder.

The broken rope sliced through the air like a sword, passing within inches of Joel's head. Workers tumbled from the ramp like beans pouring from a kettle. The remaining workers released the ropes and scrambled to safety.

The block of stone rolled backward, creeping for a second

or two and then seemingly leaping down the ramp. One of the youthful workers behind the block caught his foot on a roller and went down. His scream of terror was abruptly silenced as the enormous block rolled over him, crushing him instantly. Once it left the rollers, the block ground to a stop just as one corner struck a scaffold, knocking it loose from its moorings. Several workers tumbled to the ground.

Amazingly, additional injuries were few and most of those were minor. The work came to a halt as the slaves at the scene of the accident stood staring, stunned by the tragedy they had just witnessed. Vardaman was on the scene within moments, cracking his whip and shouting, "Keep working! Keep working! Have you never seen a dead body before?"

Within minutes, the overseers had reassigned the workers to new tasks while the engineers figured out what to do to get the block of marble back onto the rollers. Joel was given the task of carrying mortar in a wooden box.

"Make sure it is filled to the top each time," the overseer told him. "I don't want to see you carrying any half loads. Take it to the top of the ramp there, pick up an empty, and bring it back here to be refilled."

Joel lifted the mortar box, grunting with the effort. Gritting his teeth against the throbbing pain in his thigh, he struggled to carry the heavy load up the ramp. Upon reaching his destination with the loaded mortar box, he bent his knees and set it down, and then paused to catch his breath before picking up the empty one. The stinging lash of a whip caught him in the side. Startled, he looked up to see an irate overseer towering over him. "Idle wretch, keep moving!" the man snarled. Joel nodded and grabbed the empty box.

Within minutes his tunic was soaked with sweat and he was gasping for breath. His body trembled with exhaustion. The life of a fisherman can be strenuous and Joel was accustomed to hard work, but this task was grueling.

Wiping the sweat from his eyes, he bent over to pick up the loaded mortar box and began yet another trip up the ramp. "Joel! I didn't know you were here." Joel was startled when Micah appeared at his elbow. "How is your leg?"

"It's not my leg I'm worried about," Joel replied with a tired grin, pausing for a moment of rest. "It's my whole body."

"I've never worked so hard in my life," Micah agreed. He bent to pick up his own mortar box.

"It's good to see a friendly face," Joel said.

An overseer started toward them, raising his whip in warning. "Keep working."

"Maybe we can talk tonight," Micah said quickly and then hurried away with his load.

By the day's end, Joel was so thoroughly exhausted that he staggered as he left the work site with the other slaves. His entire body ached, and spasms of pain shot through his injured leg again and again. The heavy leg irons chafed his ankles. When the slaves reached the pecan grove, Joel sank to the ground with a grateful sigh. He struggled to keep his eyes open as he gulped the scanty meal that was thrust into his hands.

Desperate for sleep, he curled up on the ground beneath the pecan trees. As he closed his eyes, the scream of the dying slave echoed in his memory and the image of the runaway block of marble made him shudder with horror. *It would have been better if that were me,* he thought drowsily. *I don't know how much more of this I can take.*

Drawing his arms close to his chest in an effort to stay warm, he allowed sleep to relieve him of his misery.

Chapter Thirteen

A small fishing vessel slipped into the huge harbor, dwarfed by the tall, stately merchant ships that graced the wharves and plied the waterways. The man at the tiller was haggard, moving in the slow, methodic manner of a man who is thoroughly exhausted. His companion, a white-haired man standing at the masthead, seemed equally worn. A casual observer would have known at a glance that the cog had just traveled a great distance.

"So this is Corthia." The man at the mast scanned the harbor with interest, taking in the great ships, the wide waterways of the harbor, and the impressive skyline of the city.

The man at the tiller nodded without speaking.

The man at the mast spoke again. "Where do we start?"

"I don't really know. We don't really know if he is even in the city, and if he is, how do we go about finding him?"

The older man released a line, dropping the sail. "His Majesty knows where he is, Cobby."

Cobby nodded wearily. "I know, Pa. The first thing we must do after tying up is to send a petition."

The *Princess* glided smoothly to the dock. Wynn scrambled nimbly up the ladder with a line in his hand, only to be met at the dock by a stern-faced soldier. "What are you doing, old man?"

Wynn was startled but was not intimidated by the soldier. "Just preparing to tie off, sir."

"Do you have a Corthian certificate?"

Wynn was confused. "Sir?"

"No one moors in the harbor without a certificate of authorization from the Corthian Port Authority," the soldier said gruffly. "I assume that you don't have one."

"I didn't know we needed one," Wynn replied slowly. "How do we get one?"

"It will cost you a hundred karvas or twenty percent of your cargo," the man replied. "Seeing that you are empty, I guess that leaves you no choice but the hundred karvas."

"One hundred?" Wynn echoed. "That's outrageous, sir."

The soldier shrugged. "So tell that to the Port Authority. I don't set the fees. But unless you show me your certificate, you don't tie off here."

Wynn scrambled back down the short ladder and stepped aboard the *Princess*. "They want a hundred karvas for a certificate or they won't let us moor here."

"I heard," Cobby replied.

Wynn glanced up at the soldier. "What do you think we should do?"

"You and I both know that we can't afford a hundred karvas," Cobby replied in a low voice. "Let's move the *Princess* out of earshot while we discuss this."

The two men broke out the oars and moved the vessel away from the wharf and out into the middle of the harbor. "Pa, why don't you take the *Princess* out into the bay for a few hours while I nose around a bit and ask a few questions? Throw out a net or two so that it looks like you are fishing. Hopefully there's no fee for fishing off the coast of Corthia."

Wynn snorted. "The day they require a certificate for fishing will be the day that I take up another line of work."

Pa laughed. "You and me both."

Wynn scanned the city skyline and then looked back at Cobby. "What are you thinking of doing, Son?"

Cobby shrugged. "Joel's somewhere in this city, Pa; I'm almost sure of it, but finding him will be almost impossible."

"If there's a million people here, there's probably half a million slaves," Wynn remarked.

Cobby nodded. "I know. That's what makes it so hard. How do you search for one slave among half a million?" He sighed. "The only thing I know to do is to send a petition to His Majesty, asking for his guidance in this quest. And then I plan to go ashore and ask a few questions."

"Do you have a certificate of inquiry?" Wynn asked, keeping a straight face.

Cobby frowned. "A what?"

"You might need a permit here just to ask questions," Wynn explained with a grin.

Cobby laughed. "Let's hope not." He stepped to the small cupboard at the stern, took out a package wrapped in oilcloth, and removed a leather-bound book. Opening the book, he took out a parchment and then wrote the following message:

"My Lord, King Emmanuel:

Pa and I humbly ask your help as we seek to find my son and rescue him from this vile city. Guide us to him and enable us to release him from his chains. I would ask that you would encourage Joel and remind him that he belongs to you.

Your grateful son,

Cobby of Seawell."

Rolling the parchment tightly, the rugged fisherman raised his hand and released the petition, watching as it soared skyward. Tears streamed down his face as he turned to his father. "I'll go ashore and nose around, ask a few questions, see what I can learn about the slave trade here. Why don't you come back for me in about three hours? You can pick me up at this wharf."

The *Princess* had drifted close to a dock so the men rowed close enough for Cobby to step ashore. Cobby gripped his father's shoulder briefly and then climbed up the ladder. "Keep sending petitions, Pa. I'll see you in three hours."

Wynn nodded. "Be careful, Son." Hoisting the sail, he steered the *Princess* out into the broad watercourse heading for the open sea.

Cobby took a deep breath and then strode slowly down the busy wharf. His mind raced. *Where should I start? How will I find my son in a city of a million people? What if Joel is not even in Corthia?*

He came to a broad boulevard and stood for a moment, overwhelmed at the sight of the tall, stately buildings, the elegant carriages, the exorbitant trappings on the horses. Corthia was like no other city he had ever seen. He studied the people around him, noticing the elegant clothing and the gaudy display of jewelry and then turning away in disgust at the immodest display of flesh that paraded past him. He cringed as he heard coarse and vulgar language from the mouths of some of the most stylish of folk.

He turned back to the wharf. A well-dressed merchant stood to one side, intently watching the unloading of a tall cargo ship. Cobby approached him hesitantly. "Excuse me, sire."

The merchant turned and then gave Cobby a look of disdain. "What is it, man?" Clearly, the man considered himself Cobby's superior.

"This is my first visit to Corthia," Cobby said, feeling very ill at ease in the man's presence. "What can you tell me about the slave trade here?"

"The slave trade?" The merchant stepped back and looked Cobby over. "Are you a slaver?"

"Nay, sir." Cobby nervously licked his lips. "I've always heard that Corthia is one of the centers of the slave trade."

"What of it?"

Cobby realized that the man was growing agitated and suddenly wished that he had not started the conversation. "I—I just wondered how many slaves are sold here each week," he stammered. "Where do the slaves come from? How many slave markets are there in Corthia?"

The merchant stepped closer and studied Cobby with a suspicious glint in his eye. "Why all the questions, fisherman?" he demanded. "What are you after?"

"Nothing, sire," Cobby replied. "Have a very pleasant day, sire." He moved away quickly.

Perhaps I can simply ask directions to the slave markets without arousing suspicions, he told himself as he strode along the busy wharf, dodging carts and pedestrians as he walked. *Perhaps it is there that I will learn something about Joel's whereabouts.* He glanced back at the ill-tempered merchant and was dismayed to see that the man was talking with two soldiers.

As Cobby watched, one of the soldiers abruptly turned and looked at him, nudged his companion, and then both men strode briskly in his direction. Cobby panicked. Ducking behind a passing cargo wagon, he pushed his way through a small crowd of beggars and then scurried into a narrow side street. Walking as fast as he dared without drawing attention to himself, he turned a corner and found himself in an open market. His heart pounded as he scanned the market, trying to decide the best course of action. Most likely the soldiers were not pursuing him, but he couldn't afford to take any chances.

Hoping to blend in with the crowd, he approached a fruit vendor's cart, and, dropping his head, pretended to examine the merchandise. "May I help you, sir?"

Cobby looked up at the scowling vendor. "Just looking, sir."

"Move along, then," the vendor barked. "Peasants are not my favorite customers."

Keeping a sharp eye out for the two soldiers, Cobby slipped from the market and sauntered down the busy street, trying to look as casual as possible. He glanced over his shoulder from time to time, but saw no sign of the soldiers. After several blocks, he decided that he had eluded them. *Perhaps they weren't after me anyway,* he told himself.

He approached two men who were busily loading a freight wagon. "Excuse me, sirs. Can you tell me how to find the slave market?"

The men paused and looked him over. "The slave market?" one echoed. "Which one?"

Cobby shrugged, unsure how to answer. "Uh, the closest one, I guess."

"Looking to buy a slave, are you?"

Cobby nodded. "Aye, I am looking for a slave."

The man turned and pointed. "You're heading in the right direction. Just about a block from here, on the left. You can't miss it."

"Thank you, sir," Cobby replied. The men had already gone back to their loading.

His heart was pounding furiously as he approached the slave market, a large walled area that fronted on the harbor. As he passed through the gates he met a merchant coming out. "Is this the slave market?" he asked, scanning the arena but seeing that it was empty.

"That it is," the man replied. "We don't open until later this afternoon."

"Do you work here, sire?"

"Aye, I'm one of the auctioneers," the man replied. He looked Cobby over with an amused expression. "Are you looking to make a purchase, sir?"

"Actually, I'm looking for a particular slave," Cobby told him. "Sixteen years old, tall and skinny, bright red hair. You might have sold him within the last two weeks."

The man snorted. "We sell hundreds a day, sir. I wouldn't remember him if we sold him yesterday." His eyes abruptly narrowed and he looked at Cobby suspiciously. "Why the interest in that one slave, sir? What do you want to know?"

Suddenly Cobby realized the dangerous situation in which he had placed himself. "Perhaps I have the wrong market, sire," he said quickly. "Are there any other markets nearby?"

The auctioneer nodded, but his face revealed the fact that he was still was very suspicious of Cobby. He pointed. "Four blocks from here you'll see the Commerce Authority building. Tall structure on the right with big white pillars and a portico of black marble—you can't miss it. The slave market is behind it."

Cobby thanked him and hurried away. Moments later he spotted the Commerce Authority building and strode quickly toward it. His heart pounded furiously as he slipped around behind the imposing structure to find himself in a huge, open courtyard. At one side was a large, raised platform; on either side of that, two large fenced-off areas. A chill swept over him as he stopped and surveyed the area. *I wonder if Joel was here. Could he*—Cobby's eyes filled with tears—*could he have been sold as a slave here? Oh, my son, my son.*

The slave market was deserted. A gusting wind swept through the empty courtyard just then, lifting dust and debris and hurling it in Cobby's face as he walked slowly toward the auction block. Feeling that he was being watched, he glanced over his shoulder but saw no one. He paused, scanning the courtyard, the platform, and the holding compounds, but the entire arena was empty.

Hearing the sounds of a commotion from the platform area, he hurried toward it. "Leave me alone!" a young voice cried, and he stepped around the corner of the platform to find three young ruffians beating a younger boy. The boy was fighting bravely, but his lip was cut and his face was bruised and bloodied. He was obviously getting the worst of it.

"Enough of this!" Cobby shouted, darting forward. "Leave this boy alone!"

The three assailants paused and looked at Cobby. "This is none of your affair, sir," one of them snarled. "Be off with you."

Cobby advanced toward the youths who stood with fists clenched as he approached. "Why are you thrashing this lad?" Cobby demanded. "What has he done?"

"This doesn't concern you," the tallest youth snarled, "so stay out of it."

Cobby doubled up his fists and moved forward. "I've fought bigger, tougher foes than any of you," he told the three. "Now leave this boy alone and clear out or I'll thrash all three of you."

The tall ruffian's eyes widened as he realized that the stout fisherman meant business. Without another word he turned and fled. His two companions hesitated for the barest instant and then followed him.

"Thank you, sir," the lad said, wiping his bloody lip with the back of his hand. "I am grateful for your help."

"I was glad to do it," Cobby told him. "Why were they after you?"

"I was sweeping up when they jumped me. I told them that I didn't have any money but they didn't believe me." He turned and picked up a broom which was lying behind him. "If you hadn't come when you did, there's no telling what they would have done."

"Why didn't you use the broom?"

"I would have, but they caught me off guard," the boy replied. "I'll be ready for them next time."

Cobby glanced at the broom. "Do you work here?"

"Aye."

"Is this the slave market?"

"Aye, one of them."

"Do you work here when the slaves are sold?"

The boy nodded. "I keep the gate and I help with the tally records."

Cobby took a deep breath. "I'm looking for a young man who might have been sold here in the last two weeks. He's tall and skinny and has the brightest red hair you've ever seen."

The boy looked up at him in surprise. "Joel?"

Cobby was stunned. His heart leaped and he trembled uncontrollably as he asked, "Do you know him? Lad, have you seen my son?" Tears flooded his eyes.

The boy nodded. "Aye, sir. Joel was sold right here less than two weeks ago."

Cobby's heart pounded furiously. "Tall and skinny? Bright red hair?"

"Aye, sir. He told me that his name was Joel. I told him my name was Zachary."

Cobby began to sob. "Oh thank you, Zachary. Thank you. This is the best news I've ever heard." The tears streamed down his face unnoticed. "Do you know where he was taken? Who bought him?"

Zachary sighed. "That part is not good news, sir. He was bought by the cruelest man in Corthia. A steward named Vardaman."

Cobby began to tremble. "Where would I find him? Zachary, do you know where they took him?"

"Vardaman works for the wealthiest landowner in Corthia," he answered. "His name is Lord Tarak. He owns a huge estate on the east side of the city."

"How would I find it, lad?"

"It's called 'Chamac' sir, but all I know is that it's on the east side."

"Thank you, Zachary, thank you. You have given me new hope."

"Thank you for saving me from the beggars, sir. I hope you find your son."

"Oh, I will, I will," Cobby replied. "Good day, lad." He turned away.

"Sir?"

Cobby turned to face the lad.

"Chamac is a day's travel from here, sir."

Cobby nodded. "I've already come many times that far." He hurried toward the entrance to the slave market. *Praise Emmanuel!* he thought. *I need to tell Pa the good news and then make plans to find this Chamac place.*

As Cobby exited the slave market, a strong hand grabbed his wrist and he turned to stare into the stern faces of the two soldiers he had eluded earlier. His heart sank.

"Stranger, we're told that you are a little too inquisitive for a visitor. You've been asking quite a few questions. Perhaps we can answer your questions for you." Both men moved in so close that they were nearly touching Cobby and he noticed that both had their hands on the hilts of their swords.

He took a deep breath and shook his head. "I was just curious about Corthia's slave trade. Nothing in particular."

"Ask your questions."

Cobby's heart pounded. "I'm curious as to how many slaves are sold in Corthia each week."

The soldiers glanced at each other. "Why do you need to know that?"

Cobby shrugged. "Just curious."

"You're a fisherman, aren't you?"

"Aye."

"So why all the interest in our slave trade? Are you thinking of becoming a slaver?" The soldier's companion laughed at this.

Cobby shook his head nervously.

"Where are you from?"

"Seawell."

"Where's that?"

"You wouldn't have heard of it," Cobby replied. "Just a small fishing town...quite a ways from here."

"How far?" the soldier demanded.

It was then that Cobby made his greatest mistake. "More than a thousand miles, I reckon."

"A thousand miles?" The soldier leaned in close. "Why are you here?"

Cobby took a deep breath. *I can't tell him that I came to rescue my son from slavery,* he thought desperately. *What can I tell him?* He shrugged. "Just came to see Corthia."

The man glared at him. "Stranger, are you telling me that you sailed more than a thousand miles just to see Corthia? Surely you don't expect me to believe that. Now—what did you come for?"

Cobby was trembling but he did his best to hide it. "I have

been told that Corthia is the center of the slave trade. I just wanted to see it for myself and ask a few questions."

The soldier seemed to relax at this. "Why didn't you say so?" he asked with a friendly grin. "What can we help you with?" He lowered his hand from his sword and Cobby noticed that the hilt was adorned with gleaming blue stones.

Cobby was surprised at the abrupt change in the man's demeanor. "Is it true that Corthia is the center of the slave trade?" he asked.

"It sure is," the man replied proudly. "More slaves are bought and sold here than in any other city on the face of Terrestria."

"How many?"

"Somewhere between five and ten thousand a week."

"Between five and ten thousand," Cobby echoed, suddenly overwhelmed at the enormity of his task. Without Zachary's help there would have been no way he could have hoped to track Joel in a market of that magnitude.

"Any other questions?" the soldier asked quietly.

"I would imagine that the slaves are sold at auction?"

The man nodded. "Aye, usually."

"How many different auctions are there?"

"Slave auctions are held at five different locations throughout the city," the captain replied cordially. "The largest is located just a few blocks from here."

Cobby began to relax. "Do they keep records of the slaves that are sold? Is there any way to track the slaves from a particular location?"

"Aye, they do. Would you like to see those records?"

"Could I?" Cobby was astounded that the man would make such an offer.

He was stunned when the soldier abruptly drew his sword. "Stranger, you've been asking far too many questions for your own good. Methinks that you are an Araban spy."

"A spy?" Cobby began to tremble. "I assure you, sire, I am not a spy."

Both men suddenly seized him and before he knew what was happening, they had him in irons. "Off to the dungeon with you then," the captain told him cheerfully. "You'll have plenty of company, for you'll share a cell with other Araban spies. I suppose that some of them have been down there eight or ten years. The dungeon is known as the living death."

Chapter Fourteen

Joel lay awake in the darkness, quietly watching the two snarling boar hounds dig away relentlessly at the iron fence surrounding the sleeping slaves. The dogs had been at the task for nearly an hour and still showed no signs of letting up. *What would happen if they ever got inside?* Joel wondered. *They act as if they would eat one of us alive.*

He rolled over on his side, gritting his teeth against the pain that resulted. The wounds in his thigh were slowly healing, though not properly, and he now knew that he would walk with a limp for the rest of his life as a result of his participation in the Dragon Tournament. It seemed that every inch of his body hurt. The work on the enormous temple was brutal and he had suffered numerous minor injuries, including a sprained ankle and a dislocated shoulder. Days had turned into weeks and he had lost hope of ever sleeping in his own bed again.

His attention was drawn back to the fence as one of the boar hounds began chewing at the iron bars that separated him from his sleeping quarry. A deep growl rumbled in his throat. Joel shuddered.

"Joel!" The exhausted young slave jumped in fright as his name was whispered in his ear. "Joel, are you awake?"

"I am now, Micah," Joel replied in a whisper. "What do you want?"

"If I tried to escape, would you go with me?"

"What?" Joel was stunned by the question.

"If I tried to escape, would you go with me?"

"I heard you the first time," Joel replied, scooting closer to Micah to avoid being overheard by the guard, who stood on the opposite end of the enclosure, twenty paces away. "I can't believe you're asking me this. I thought we agreed we weren't going to talk about it any more."

"I can't help it," Micah replied. "Joel, we have to try! I can't take much more of this."

"Neither can I," Joel whispered fiercely, "but it won't do us any good talking about trying to escape. You and I both know that escape from Chamac is impossible."

"There has to be a way," Micah insisted. "We have to try."

"Micah, listen! Escape is impossible, and we both know it. We wear leg irons at all times. During the day the overseers watch us so closely that we can't even scratch without them knowing about it, and guards are posted at the gates with orders to kill any slave who attempts to escape. At night we're chained together like wild beasts and there are killer dogs prowling the grounds, anxious to devour any slave foolish enough to try to run for it. Look at the dogs at the fence, Micah. They'd eat you alive if you weren't inside this enclosure!"

Joel took a deep breath. "So—what's your plan, clever boy? If you have one, I want to hear it."

"I don't have a plan yet—" Micah began, but Joel cut him off.

"You don't have a plan and you never will!" he whispered fiercely. "There is no escape from this wretched place! Escape would be impossible and we'd just get ourselves killed if we tried it. So why don't you just put the idea out of your foolish little head and quit talking about it?"

"We can't just give up," Micah retorted. "If we give up we just die here."

"I don't see what else we can do," Joel said bitterly. "There is no way to escape Chamac and talking about it doesn't help anything. All it does is just make us both more miserable."

"If we talk about it maybe we can come up with a workable plan."

"There is no workable plan!" Joel growled. "We both know that. The only way that an escape would even be remotely possible is if we had some outside help, and who's going to do that?"

"But there has to be a way."

The guard lifted his torch and moved in their direction.

"Go to sleep, Micah. We can talk again tomorrow."

Cobby awoke slowly. He stretched and opened his eyes, looking around drowsily as he tried to make sense of his surroundings. He was lying in a poorly lit subterranean chamber, surrounded by walls of mud. Suddenly, memory sharpened and his heart sank when he recalled what had happened.

After being interrogated by the soldiers the night before for nearly two hours, he had been whipped and then lowered into this loathsome pit that served as a dungeon. He sat up and looked around. It had been dark when he was brought here, and he now surveyed his surroundings with a growing sense of dismay. Nearly thirty feet across, the primitive dungeon was simply a hole in the ground with walls of mud that curved inward and upward to the tiny opening twenty feet above him, the only source of light. The chamber was shaped like the inside of a giant bottle. Hearing the splash and gurgle of running water, he looked down at the floor where a swift stream flowed across the chamber to disappear under the base of the wall. The air reeked of death and decay.

"The new lad's awake," a voice said, and the comment was greeted by a round of coarse laughter.

Still trying to adjust his eyes to the dim light, Cobby stared into the darkness to see nearly a score of gaunt figures sitting or lying about the cave. He stared. Prisoners like himself, these men were the most pitiful wretches he had ever seen, with sunken eyes, skeletal limbs, and tattered shreds of clothing clinging to their wasted bodies. Their hair was long and caked and matted and their beards were long and unkempt, like gardens abandoned to the weeds and briars. He could tell at a glance that most of them had skin diseases.

"What's your name?" The speaker was a tall man, incredibly thin, with a filthy gray beard that reached nearly to his waist. He stood before Cobby, eyes wild and staring, vigorously scratching his side.

Cobby licked his lips nervously. "Cobby. Cobby of Seawell."

"Forget Seawell, Cobby of Seawell, for you'll never see it again. You are now Cobby of Corthia." The tall man abruptly threw back his head and screamed with laughter.

A thin hand tapped Cobby on the arm and he turned to realize that a prisoner was seated right beside him. "Don't pay Simon any mind," the man said. "His mind is gone. He thinks he's the governor of Corthia." He pointed across the room to a man on his knees who repeatedly banged his head against the clay floor. "Anselm there is almost as bad."

Cobby nodded.

The man extended a hand. "I'm Levi. As far as I know, I still have most of my mind." He smiled sadly as Cobby shook his hand. "At times, I almost think it would be better to be like Simon or Anselm."

Cobby took a deep breath. "Is there any way out of here?" His question was greeted by howls of laughter and he realized too late just how foolish he had sounded.

Levi lowered his voice. "We don't talk about that. The only entrance to this wretched place is the opening overhead, and as you can see, it's at least twenty feet above us."

Cobby fought against a rising sense of panic. "How long— how long have these men been down here?"

"You can tell who's been here the longest by the length of their beards," Levi replied in a low voice. "Anselm has been here the longest; he was here several years before me."

"How—how long have you been here?"

"I can't really tell you. When I was first thrown down here I kept track of the days, but I quit when I reached the four-year mark. That was several years ago."

"Several years ago?" Cobby was horrified. "But when will you get out?"

Levi shook his head. "There is no way out of here, my friend. We call this place 'mortis vivus,' which means 'living death.' When you've been here for awhile you'll understand what we mean. One long, dreary day runs into the next, day after day, month after month, year after year, with no end in sight. I'm telling you, it's worse than death."

Cobby hesitated. "What did you do?"

Levi laughed. "To get myself thrown in here, you mean? Nothing, really. I inadvertently insulted the governor at a din- ner party. Next thing I know, I'm being tossed in here." He gestured at the other men around the dim chamber. "It's the same with nearly every man here. Some have been charged with spying for the Arabians; one was thrown in here because he refused to sell his property to a magistrate; a merchant was thrown in because he attempted to sell a slave without going through the slave market. Thomas there was a guard at the governor's palace, but he was thrown in when he refused to kill an innocent man."

Cobby struggled to breathe. "But what happens when you stand before a magistrate?" he asked. "Surely if a man is innocent the charges against him are dropped."

Levi shook his head. "You are in Corthia, my friend. There will be no chance to stand before a magistrate. Once you are down here, you are beyond hope."

"But I did nothing wrong!" Cobby protested. "I asked a few questions about the Corthian slave trade. The next thing I know, I'm in chains being interrogated, and then suddenly I'm being dumped in here." He grabbed Levi's arm in a desperate grip. "I have to get out of here, Levi. I have to! My son is somewhere in this cursed city and I have to find him! He was sold as a slave, sir."

Levi shook his head. "You'll never get out, Cobby, and you could never hope to find him if you could get out. Do your best to forget him."

"Forget him?" Cobby echoed. "How can a man forget his own son? I would die for him! I have to get out. I must find him, must go to him, must set him free and get him out of this wretched city!"

Levi held up one hand as if to calm him. "There is no way out of here, my friend, and if you allow yourself to dwell on your son's predicament, you will go mad. Far better to simply forget him."

"How do you know there's no way out?" Cobby protested, looking from one man to another as if to make an appeal. "Has anyone tried to escape this place?"

"There's only one way out," another prisoner told him, pointing to the far end of the dark chamber. "There."

Cobby turned and stared into the darkness and at last could make out several mounds of dirt. He shuddered as the meaning of the man's words sank in. A nagging thought pushed its way to the front of his mind and he turned to Levi. "Do they feed us?"

Levi shrugged. "Every day or two someone will throw scraps of garbage down to us," he replied slowly. "I'll tell you before it happens, my friend—you have to fight for what you get." He gestured toward the watercourse. "The stream provides us with plenty of fresh water and carries away our garbage and our waste. Drink all you want, but don't expect much to eat."

"I will find a way out of here," Cobby vowed. "There is a way out, and I will find it. I must get to my son."

Levi just shook his head sadly.

"He's a slave, sir!" Cobby blurted, seizing Levi's skeletal arm without realizing it. "Joel is a slave, and I will do whatever it takes to find him."

"Others have tried, Cobby," Levi replied quietly. "You are in here for good, and the sooner you realize that, the better off you will be."

"I will find a way," Cobby replied fiercely. "I will find a way or die trying."

"Then die you will, my friend," Levi told him sadly. "There is no escape from mortis vivus."

Just then there was a shout of anger and the sounds of a struggle. Cobby looked over to see several men fighting in the darkness and realized that someone had dropped some garbage down into the dungeon. The prisoners were fighting over it. He turned to Levi. "I didn't even see it coming."

Levi nodded. "After you've been here awhile, you'll almost learn to anticipate it. If you don't, you'll do without."

Cobby stood stiffly to his feet and stepped over to the stream. The water flowed through an iron grate spanning a dark opening at the base of the wall. "Where does the stream go?"

"Forget the stream if you're thinking of escaping," Levi warned him. "No one knows where it goes—it simply flows down into the heart of Terrestria. Only a fool would try to swim out, for he would drown long before he found air. Anyway, there is a grate installed that keeps us from even trying it." He laughed. "Corthia doesn't want to lose her prisoners—not even to death."

The next morning, Joel was in line with the other slaves waiting for the usual meager breakfast when a tall overseer strode up to him and barked, "Come with me."

Joel's heart pounded with fear. "W-what have I done, s-sir?"

"Nothing yet," the man growled. "I have a job for you."

"I haven't eaten yet, sir."

"You'll eat tonight," the man retorted. With a sinking heart, Joel followed him. *This will be a long day without food,* he told himself. *It's almost impossible to work hard enough to satisfy these cruel taskmasters, even with a full belly.*

The overseer paused beside a freight wagon. "Climb on," he ordered. "You're going into town with me." He pointed to several other young slaves nearby. "Come along."

Moments later the freight wagon rolled through the front gates of Chamac with the overseer seated on the spring seat and a dozen slaves in back. A strange feeling swept over Joel. *This is the first time I've been outside the grounds since coming to*

Corthia. What if I could somehow escape while we are in the city?

Fifteen minutes later the wagon crossed the bridge suspended above the narrow canyon he had seen on the way to
Chamac. Joel stood to his feet in the back of the wagon to get
a better look and the overseer noticed. Reaching back with
one hand, the man grabbed Joel's chain and jerked his feet out
from under him. Joel landed heavily on his side, knocking the
wind out of him. "Don't even try it," the man growled.

"I—I wasn't going to jump, sir," Joel stammered, struggling
painfully to draw a breath. "I just wanted to see the canyon."

"You wouldn't be the first if you did," came the reply. "More
than one slave has jumped from this bridge."

Joel shuddered as he imagined the long, terrifying drop that
would result from such a leap: the horror of falling, falling,
falling...the terror of seeing the ground rushing up to meet
you...the horrible impact as one's body struck the rocks at the
bottom of the chasm...*How could anyone end his own life in such
a way?*

The slave beside him seemed to read his mind. "I'd jump in
an instant if I had the chance," he whispered. "Better to die
than to spend the rest of one's miserable life working for Lord
Tarak, eh?"

Joel didn't answer. The wagon crossed the bridge and continued down the slope. Shaken by the thought of a fall into the canyon, Joel trembled. His thoughts turned to his home at Seawell
and the better days he had once known. *I wonder if Pa and Papa
Wynn are out fishing on the Princess right now. Does Pa ever think of
me? I would give anything just to hear his voice once more. . . .*

The image of his mother's kind face appeared on the walls of
his memory and his eyes filled with tears. *I wonder what Ma thought
when she learned that I had been taken. How often does she think of me? If
only I could see her for just a moment or two!*

Some time later the wagon rolled down a wide boulevard in the business district of Corthia and stopped in the center of a huge plaza in the shadow of an enormous statue of a mounted knight. A soldier in chain mail approached the wagon. "Lord Tarak's contribution to the Festival," the overseer told him. "I'll return for them this evening."

The soldier nodded. "Please inform your master that the governor accepts his contribution. His property will be returned to him half an hour before sunset."

"I'll be here."

The soldier gestured to the slaves. "Climb down and stand beside the wagon," he ordered. The slaves complied. "Today you are under my authority," he told them. "You'll find pails and scrub brushes at the base of the statue of Olempas the Magnificent, the founder of the great city of Corthia. You'll work in pairs. You're to scrub the cobblestones of the plaza in preparation for the Festival of Wealth."

With a taunting grin, the soldier produced a whip. "I need not remind you that you are here to work. If I suspect that you are not working your hardest, even for a moment, you'll get a taste of the whip, and believe me, I know how to draw blood with the first lash." He paused and looked each slave directly in the eye one by one. "Every entrance to the plaza is secured, but should any slave be foolish enough to attempt an escape, the result will be a quick but painful death."

He produced a key. "Let's get you paired off and get you working."

Five minutes later Joel was on his hands and knees with dozens of other slaves, all vigorously scrubbing the cobblestones with crude scrub brushes and pails of soapy water. The chain of each slave's leg irons had been passed through that of another slave, linking the slaves together in pairs to thwart any attempt at escape.

Joel's partner stopped for a moment to wipe the sweat from his eyes. "I don't think I can keep this up all day," he complained. "This is rough! By tonight my knees will be nothing but bloody stumps."

"Keep working," Joel urged in a whisper. "If they catch you slacking they'll whip you."

The admonition came too late. A nearby overseer noticed the brief interlude and strode over. The whip lashed out to strike the young slave, opening a small gash in his side. With a second crack of the whip, he raised a welt on Joel's hip. "Keep working!" he raged. "I want to see those brushes moving, moving, moving!"

Moments later, Joel bumped shoulders with another slave, a young girl with long, dark hair. "I'm sorry," he said in a low voice, glancing toward the closest overseer to make certain that he was not being observed and then continuing to scrub furiously. "I didn't mean to bump you."

"It's all right," the girl responded, and Joel jerked his head up in amazement.

"Myra!"

The girl was just as startled as he. "Joel!"

Joel glanced at the overseer. "Myra, are you all right? Where are you living?"

"You were sold to Lord Tarak, weren't you?" she responded.

Joel nodded. "The meanest man in Corthia."

"Well, I was sold to his son, Belosi. He owns the estate right next to Lord Tarak's and he's just as cruel as his father."

Keeping their heads low, the two friends continued to talk as they worked. "Why are we scrubbing the cobblestones as if this were a palace floor?" Joel asked.

Myra looked at him. "Haven't you heard about the Festival?"

Joel shook his head. "Not a word."

"From what I've heard, it's an annual event, and it's the biggest thing in Corthia. Three days of feasting, jousting, and tournaments. Minstrels and jesters and magicians. Contenders come from all parts of Terrestria to compete in the tournaments."

"And we're going to scrub the entire city in preparation," Joel groaned.

Myra shrugged. "Probably."

"When does it start?"

"In about a week, I think. Belosi's people have been making preparations for weeks. The whole thing starts with a giant parade in which the lords of Corthia display their power and their wealth, showing off their horses, their garrisons of knights, and their slaves. They say it's really something to see, for each lord decks his household out in the colors of his heraldry. Belosi's is blue and purple. Lord Tarak's is blue and yellow, I believe."

Scrubbing furiously, Joel glanced at the overseer. "So you and I are going to be marching in a parade wearing the colors of our masters just to add to the pageantry?"

Myra nodded. "Isn't it exciting?"

Joel lifted his head and stared at her. "We're slaves, Myra. What does it matter? I'm not that excited at the idea of being paraded around town as the property of Lord Tarak."

"It's the one day of the year when these wretched shackles will be taken off our ankles," she told him, and her eyes filled with tears. "And I'm told that we will feast with all the others."

"I'll get excited when I hear that they're going to take off the shackles for good," Joel growled. An overseer began making his way toward them just then, so Joel and his partner moved away from the two girls. Moments later Myra and her partner were lost from view.

Cobby knelt at the edge of the subterranean stream, studying the grate in the dim light. Levi noticed and hurried over. "Don't even think about it, Cobby."

Cobby looked up at him. "Think about what?"

"I know what's going through your head," the other man replied. "You're wondering if you could somehow remove the grate and attempt to swim out."

"You told me there's no other way out," Cobby countered.

"Cobby, it's certain death! If you could remove the grate, you'd never swim out. The stream goes underground and who knows how far it goes before it surfaces, or even if it does surface! You would drown before you found a way out."

"The grate is rusted pretty badly," Cobby replied, as if he had not heard a word that Levi said. "If a man pulled with all his strength, he just might tear it loose."

"Cobby, listen to me—"

"Nay, you listen to me," Cobby said fiercely. "After being in here for eight years or however long you've been here, you told me that staying here is worse than death. My son is a slave, Levi. Somewhere in this cursed city, my son, Joel, is chained to a tree like an animal. I must find him and set him free."

"You'll never make it," Levi told him. "You'll drown before you find a way out."

"Then I'll die for my son," Cobby replied. He waded into the stream, flinching a bit when he felt the shock of the frigid water. Reaching down, he grasped the iron grate with both hands. "Emmanuel, my King, help me," he said softly, and then pulled upwards with all his might. To the amazement of all the prisoners, the grate pulled free, and Cobby tumbled backwards into the water. He stood to his feet, setting the iron grate on the bank of the stream.

"I beg you, Cobby, don't try it," Levi implored him.

"I will free my son or die in the attempt," the determined fisherman replied. He looked up at the ring of haggard faces surrounding the stream. "Farewell, my friends. I would wish that I could somehow find freedom for each of you."

With these parting words, Cobby took several deep breaths and then lowered his body into the rushing waters. Raising his head, he took a deep, deep breath, held it, and then plunged beneath the surface and disappeared into the darkness beyond the wall.

Chapter Fifteen

Joel lay with his back against the fence, shivering with cold and caught in the depths of despair. Micah was gone, beaten to death that afternoon by an angry overseer, and Joel had witnessed the brutal assault. The agonized screams of his friend still echoed in his ears and the look of anguish on Micah's face would be etched in Joel's memory forever.

He wept, his body convulsing with sobs. Micah's last words would haunt him for the rest of his days. Just thinking about them brought pain to his soul and reminded him of his own great loss. "Papa!" the dying slave had cried. "Papa, please help me!"

"Oh, Papa," Joel wept softly, for he saw in Micah's death a foreshadowing of his own. "Papa, help me." *Will I die here in Corthia, as Micah died? Will I ever see Papa again?*

After some time his thoughts turned to the upcoming Festival. Myra had told him that all slaves would have their leg irons removed on the day of the Festival. Was she correct? Would that afford him the chance to escape? It was too much to hope for.

Slowly he became aware of a strange presence in his immediate vicinity and he carefully opened his eyes and scanned the darkness about him, but saw no one. A large, shapeless mass of rotting vegetation lay against the fence, just inches from his face, and he stared at it for a long moment. *That wasn't there a few moments ago,* he told himself, and the hairs on the back of his neck stood straight up. *I know it wasn't there when I lay down!*

The mass moved slightly. Fear clutched at Joel's heart. His breath came in short, ragged gasps. *What is this thing?*

"Joel?"

Joel nearly screamed at the whisper of his name, but he caught himself in time to keep from crying out. Tense with fear, he lay still, heart pounding furiously. Afraid to move, he found that he could not even breathe. He could only wait. Wait and watch the mysterious mass just inches from his face.

"Joel." The mass moved again, almost imperceptibly, a movement so slight that Joel was not certain that he had not imagined it.

"Who are you? What are you?" Joel's mouth was so dry he could barely whisper the words. "What do you want with me?"

His heart leaped when he received the answer. "Joel, don't move and don't say anything for a moment. You don't want to call attention to yourself. It's me, Son. Your Pa."

"Pa?" Joel's heart seemed to stop. "Pa?"

"I'm here, Son. I came to get you out."

Joel stared at the mass of vegetation and his mind refused to accept the information he was receiving. "Pa," he whispered, "is it really you? How could you be here, Pa? That's impossible! Are you a—a spirit?"

A hand reached through the fence and touched him. "It's me, Son. Praise be to King Emmanuel, I have found you at last."

Joel grabbed the hand and clutched it to his chest as the tears flowed down his face. "Pa. Oh, Pa. I never thought I'd see you again, Pa."

The mass moved convulsively and Joel heard sobs coming from it. "I love you, Son."

"Pa, I—" Joel choked on the words. "Pa, I went to the Dragon Tournament. I—"

"I know, Son," Pa interrupted. "Don't talk about it now. You've been forgiven."

Separated by the fence, Cobby and Joel clutched each other in the darkness, sobbing together as the reality of their reunion slowly seeped into Joel's consciousness. Slowly, slowly, his despair was replaced by hope. The situation was impossible, but everything would somehow be all right. Pa was here.

Joel turned over and scanned the yard. Other slaves lay within six feet of him, but as far as he could tell they were all fast asleep. So far, his father's visit had gone unnoticed. He breathed a sigh of relief and turned back to face his father. "How did you know where to find me?"

"A young man at the auction grounds told me that you had been purchased by a wealthy landowner named Lord Tarak. For the last two days I've been watching the estate from a nearby hill through Papa Wynn's spyglass. Tonight it took me four hours to crawl half a mile from the gate."

A dog barked in the distance, and Joel's heart constricted with fear as he suddenly remembered the boar hounds prowling the darkness. "Pa, there are dogs in here! Killer dogs, Pa! They'll eat you alive! Get out of here, Pa—they'll kill you!"

The shapeless mass gave a low chuckle. "Don't worry about the dogs, Son. They won't give us any trouble."

"Pa, they're Karnivan boar hounds!" Joel whispered fiercely. "They're trained to kill! They'll catch your scent and be on you at any moment. Please, Pa—"

"Son, listen to me. Have you ever heard of karmania?"

"Nay, sir."

"It's an herb that grows in swamps. To humans it's odorless, but it drives dogs crazy. They avoid it like death. And once they catch a whiff of it, the herb seems to numb their sense of smell for hours."

"You mean they can't smell anything?" Joel whispered.

"Exactly. My concealment is made from one of the nets from the *Princess*. I wove seaweed and land plants into it to create a mass that no one would recognize as a human and saturated it with karmania to throw off the dogs."

Joel began to relax. "What are we going to do, Pa?"

"I don't know yet, Son. It will take a day of hard thinking to come up with a plan, but I want you to know that I will get you out. That's why I'm here."

"I never thought I'd have the chance to say this again, Pa, but I love you."

Cobby squeezed his arm. "I love you, Son."

"I'm sorry for what happened, Pa."

"Joel, we don't have time to talk any further. It will take me several hours to crawl back out of here—I have to move so slowly that no one sees any movement. It's an old trick I learned from the Nidians." He squeezed Joel's arm once more. "I'll be back with an escape plan tomorrow night, Son."

Joel awoke the next morning with a feeling that something was about to happen. He rubbed his eyes, trying to determine why he had this sense of anticipation, this aura of excitement. He thought about the Festival. It was only three days away, yet that in itself would not have created this air of expectancy, this feeling that something great was about to happen. It had to be something else.

He turned toward the fence, and then it hit him. Pa had been here! Pa had found him! He let out his breath in a long sigh of satisfaction. It was unbelievable, totally beyond the realm of possibility, but last night he had talked with his father. Cobby of Seawell had somehow tracked him all the way to Corthia.

What if I merely dreamed it? The thought hit him like a fist between the eyes. *Seawell is more than a thousand miles from here! Pa could not possibility have tracked me to Corthia, and even if he did, he could never have found me in this huge city.* Disappointment swept over him, crushing in its intensity. He studied the fence line, looking for evidence that his father had been there, but found nothing. In his desperate plight, his imagination had created a ray of hope for him, but in the reality of daylight the dream faded like a phantom of the night.

He sighed. The dream had been so real. Pa had been there at the fence, talking to him, touching him! He had heard Pa's voice; he had felt Pa's strong grip. "I'll be back with a plan tomorrow night, Son." The words of the promise echoed in his memory and he struggled again with reality. *Was Pa really here, or did I merely dream it?*

For a moment he lay still as he relived the details of Pa's visit. Real or imagined, Pa's presence brought solace to his lonely heart. He had been with Pa, if only in a dream. But the dream had been so real, so encouraging. "I'll be back. . . ." The words were a feast of hope to his hungry soul and he clung to them desperately

A quick blow to the side of the head brought him back to the cruel realities of the present. "Slave—on your feet!" a harsh voice barked. "Get moving!" Joel leaped to his feet as all thoughts of Pa vanished like soap bubbles.

The day was hard. Joel and a dozen others spent several hours digging a drainage trench from the barn to the creek. Somehow the overseers seemed even more cruel than usual and lashed out with their whips at the slightest provocation. By the time the sun set, Joel's entire body ached from exhaustion.

Did I really see Pa? he asked himself as he and the others trudged in from the worksite. *Was he really here, or did I just imagine it? Well, I'll know in just a few hours, when he comes back tonight. Or fails to.* He approached the slave enclosure.

He was handed a bowl of thin gruel and a flask of water. As he sat down to consume the miserly meal he was keenly aware of Micah's absence. Suddenly he felt lonelier than he had ever been in his life. Alone in a hostile land, abused on a daily basis by cruel overseers, he gave in again to a debilitating sense of discouragement.

If only Pa's visit had been real, he thought mournfully. *He promised to come back tonight, but if he wasn't really here...*

Joel stayed awake for several hours, but his father didn't return that night. Or the next.

The moon was nearly full on the night before the Festival. Surrounded by sleeping slaves, Joel lay awake. His body was exhausted from the day's work, but his mind refused to rest. *Tomorrow is the Festival that we have heard so much about. If it is true that the slaves will have their shackles removed for the festivities, will that give me an opportunity to escape? But even if it did, where would I go? How would I ever get back home to Seawell? A thousand miles is a long way to walk....*

A strange uneasiness crept over him and he sensed that he

was being watched. He turned his face toward the fence and then jumped in fright. Just beyond the fence, two feet from where he lay, the mass of rotting vegetation lay in exactly the same spot as it had two nights previous. He held his breath, paralyzed with fear, unsure of what he should do. Was this bizarre apparition his father, or was he merely dreaming?

"Joel."

The moment he heard his father's whisper, Joel knew that he was not imagining the strange visit, nor was he dreaming. Just as he had promised, his father had come back for him.

"Pa, it's so good to see you again. You came back for me."

Cobby reached through the fence and gripped his son's arm. "My heart rejoices to see you, Son. Listen closely, for we do not have much time. Tomorrow is the Corthian Festival, and therein lies our only hope for your escape; for I am told that you and the other slaves will have your leg irons replaced with wrist irons for the parades and pageantry."

He gripped Joel's arm for a few seconds and then continued. "Joel, I have a plan for your escape. It is a bold plan and depends on the element of surprise, but if the smallest thing goes wrong, we will both die tomorrow." He paused. "Will you trust me and do exactly as I say?"

Joel nodded. "Aye," he whispered.

Cobby passed a length of rope through the bars of the fence. "Pull up your tunic and tie this securely around your waist," he instructed. "Move slowly and quietly so that you do not call attention to yourself. I'll watch the others and warn you if one of them stirs."

"What is the hook for?" Joel whispered.

"Just listen as you work," his father replied. "Position the rope so that the hook end comes out the top of your tunic, right in front of your face. Understand?"

"Aye, sir." Moving slowly and cautiously, Joel began to work to follow his father's instructions.

"We both know that when you attempt to escape, you will be pursued immediately by Lord Tarak's overseers. I had to find a way to quickly put a great distance between us and your pursuers. For that reason we will make our move just before you reach the canyon bridge."

"The canyon bridge?" Joel took a deep breath as he raised his hips and passed the rope harness underneath his torso. "Pa, what are you planning?"

"I am told that it is customary for each landowner to march his slaves in tight ranks to the Festival," Cobby replied. "A parade, as it were. When you and Lord Tarak's other slaves are forming ranks, do your best to get a place in the rank to the far right. You will be wearing wrist irons, but make sure that the hook from your harness is in position to easily be pulled out the top of your tunic. Joel, the entire plan depends on that one detail."

Joel struggled to knot the rope around his waist. "I can do that."

"When Lord Tarak's cavalcade reaches a point about three furlongs from the bridge, a nobleman in blue will pass on your right side. Keep your eyes open and watch for him. He will be riding a tall black mare with white markings on the forelegs."

"Who is this nobleman?" Joel asked. "What if he doesn't come?"

"I'll be that nobleman," Cobby replied. "And believe me, I'll be there." He glanced across the slave enclosure and then continued. "When I give the signal, break rank and run to my horse. Cross behind her and approach from the right side. There won't be time to mount, so simply leap up and loop your wrist irons over the pommel of the saddle. Be sure to lift your feet.

"We'll ride about a furlong along a trail that follows the canyon, and it is at that point that we will cross the canyon. Our pursuers will be unable to follow us and thus we will make our escape."

"Wait," Joel interrupted. "Pa, how will we cross the canyon?"

"There isn't time to go into that now," Cobby replied. "But you must remember to follow my orders instantly and completely, for a moment's hesitation could mean failure and death for both of us. Son, two seconds' delay could mean disaster. We'll have to move fast, for I'm sure that our pursuers will be right on our heels. The whole plan depends on the element of surprise."

"I'll be surprised if we make it," Joel said glumly. "Pa, are you sure this will work?"

Cobby sighed. "Nay, Son, I am not. But it's the only plan I have."

"There are so many things that could go wrong, Pa."

"No one knows that better than I, Son. We'll have to trust King Emmanuel for protection."

Cobby gripped Joel's hand for a long moment. "I'll see you tomorrow, my son. Watch for me and be ready to respond to my signal. We must trust in His Majesty's protection, for without him, our escape attempt will end in failure. Good night, Son."

As Joel watched, Cobby crawled away into the darkness of the night, hugging the ground like a serpent.

Chapter Sixteen

The day of the Festival dawned bright and clear. Joel awoke with a sense of excitement and anticipation and his thoughts immediately went to the plans that his father had made. Was it possible that within a few hours he would be free of Lord Tarak and Vardaman and the cruel overseers? Was freedom actually within his grasp? *I'll know before the day is out,* he told himself. *By nightfall, I'll be free, or...dead.*

"Here, put this on." An overseer moved among the wakening slaves as he passed out colorful garments. He handed Joel a garment, took one look at Joel's height, and then took it back. "Here, try this one—it's longer. It goes on right over your tunic." He handed Joel a second garment.

Joel unfolded the item of clothing to find that it was a simple surcoat, a sleeveless, loose-fitting garment with low-cut armholes. He slipped it on and then looked up to see that the yard was a sea of blue-and-yellow as the other slaves tried on their surcoats. *We're all the property of Lord Tarak,* he thought ruefully. *Blue and yellow—the colors of cruelty.*

Servants moved through the yard with trays of food, and Joel was surprised to see that the meal consisted of hot cakes, fruit, and roast pork. He took a seat under a walnut tree and wolfed down the delicious meal. *Oh, that every day was Festival day if it would mean that we would eat like this,* he thought longingly. *I haven't had meat since I came to Corthia.*

Just as he was finishing he looked up to see a servant hovering nearby with a loaded tray. "Would you like more?"

Joel nodded eagerly. "Aye, I would, please."

When the meal was finished, two overseers with keys passed through the ranks of the slaves, removing the hated leg irons and replacing them with smaller, lighter wrist irons. About the same time, a line of ornate carriages filled with lords and ladies and members of the household rolled down the tree-lined lane that led to the main gate. As the vehicles came to a stop under the trees, Joel saw that they were gaily decorated with ribbons and bunting and fresh flowers. Behind the carriages, a cavalcade of knights in shining armor sat astride snowy white chargers. The blue and yellow banner flying grandly from the tip of each man's lance carried the same coat of arms as each of the coaches. As Joel watched, the knights dismounted and stood at attention beside their magnificent horses. The spirited chargers pranced and pawed the earth.

Vardaman rode forward on a dashing white horse. His saddle and bridle were of silver, and set with brilliant blue Corthian lapis stones. "Move out to the road," the steward called in a loud voice. "We'll assemble in ranks and prepare to march into Corthia."

The slaves moved uncertainly toward the lane. One of the young men deliberately fell against one of the young female slaves, knocking her down in the process. Joel was right behind them when it happened, and his temper flared. Grabbing the youth by the shoulder, he spun him around. "What was that for?" he demanded. "You did that on purpose!"

"Did I now?" the other replied tauntingly. "What are you

going to do about it, tall boy?"

Joel drew back his fist. "Apologize to the lady," he ordered. "Now."

The lash of a whip wrapped itself several times around Joel's wrist and then tightened abruptly, pulling Joel off balance. He spun around to find himself looking up into the angry face of Vardaman. "Slave, didn't we already deal with this problem?" the steward demanded, his eyes filled with fury. "I've told you not to jump in where you're not invited."

"Sire," Joel protested, "he was mistreating this girl. I stood up for her."

Vardaman trembled with rage. "Didn't we have this conversation before? I told you then and I'll tell you now—stay out of matters that don't concern you! Don't you understand? You are a slave, nothing more. You are not the righter of wrongs. You are not to interfere in matters involving other slaves."

"I couldn't let him mistreat her," Joel replied quietly.

Infuriated, Vardaman raised his whip and then thought better of it. "I can't bloody your clothes when we are about to go to the Festival, can I?" He paused for a moment and then grinned wickedly. "Tall boy, you're going to miss the Festival!" He turned to an overseer. "Take him back and chain him to a tree. This impertinent slave is not going to the Festival."

Stunned, Joel could only stare at the man. *You can't keep me from the Festival!* his mind cried out. *You can't! If I don't go to the Festival, I won't be able to meet Pa and I can't escape this wretched place! I have to go!*

The overseer took Joel by the arm and began to lead him back to the slave yard. Joel was close to panic. *What am I going to do? If I can't meet Pa, I'll be a slave to Lord Tarak forever!*

At that moment, a second cavalcade of knights rode up on splendid chargers, led by a tall nobleman that Joel knew to be Lord Tarak. "Vardaman," Lord Tarak called, "what is the meaning of this? Where is he taking that lad?"

"We are dealing with an impertinent slave, sire," Vardaman explained tersely. "We are taking him back to the yard—he will not attend the Festival."

Lord Tarak shook his head. "Deal with him later, Vardaman. I want all of our people at the Festival." He wheeled his horse around and led his men to a position at the rear of the procession.

Vardaman advanced on Joel, so enraged that he was shaking. "When we get back from the Festival, slave boy, I personally will beat you until you will wish that were dead. See if I don't." He wheeled his horse and rode over to join the procession.

Guided by the overseers, the slaves assembled in ranks in the narrow driveway. Joel remembered his father's instructions and managed to get a position in the far right column. Foot soldiers in chain mail took up positions on either side of the ranks of slaves. Joel studied the sword of the man nearest him and saw the familiar blue lapis stones adorning the hilt of the weapon. Courtiers with blue-and-yellow banners held aloft on staffs and trumpeters with gleaming brass trumpets took up positions at the front of the assemblage. The trumpets sounded a fanfare and then the entire procession moved through the gate and into the roadway.

The road was filled with Corthians, all on their way to the Festival of Wealth. Peasants on foot walked single file on the left side of the road while horses and carriages passed them on the right. Processions from two other estates moved proudly past Chamac while Lord Tarak's entourage waited, but Joel noticed that neither was as large or as grand as Lord Tarak's. When both processions had passed, the procession from Chamac moved into the road.

After a furlong or two Joel glanced at the soldier beside him. The man was huge. Taller than Joel, he had massive arms and shoulders that gave evidence of tremendous strength. His chiseled face was stern but his eyes were alive and exuded friendly warmth, and his curly blond hair glistened in the morning sun like spun gold. Joel glanced down at the man's sword and was surprised to see the hilt adorned with gleaming rubies rather than the blue lapis stones he had expected.

"This will be a day to remember, lad," the huge knight said quietly, and Joel looked up at him, amazed that the man would deign to speak to a slave.

"Aye, sire, that it will," Joel replied. "This is my first Festival."

"Oh, are you going to the Festival, lad? I thought your father had other plans for you." The words were spoken softly, in a jesting tone, and Joel looked up in alarm to see the keen eyes crinkled with amusement.

Joel's breath seemed to catch in his throat. "Sire," he croaked, "do you know my father?" His heart pounded furiously and he was close to panic. *How could this soldier know my father? Does he know of the escape plan?*

"Cobby of Seawell is one of the finest men alive today," the tall knight answered, "yet you have disregarded his counsel and wisdom, and instead have listened to the lies of foolish friends. Had you been as loyal to your father as he is to you, at this moment you would be home in Seawell instead of here in Corthia." He glanced at Joel, and the look was stern but not unkind. "What is that I see upon your hands?"

"Chains, sire. I am a slave to Lord Tarak."

The man nodded. "And how did they get there, lad? You are the son of one of the wisest men in Seawell, yet I find you here in Corthia as a common slave. How did this come about?"

Joel hung his head. "As you said, sire, I listened to the lies of foolish friends."

"You are in the process of learning this already, Joel, but I will say it anyway—your father and mother are the best friends you will ever have in this life. Your father would give his life for you in a heartbeat. Your grandfather would do the same."

Joel swallowed hard, and his eyes filled with tears. Not trusting himself to speak, he simply nodded. He glanced around at the other slaves marching along with him, but not one paid him any attention. It was as if they had not heard even a word of the conversation.

"Lad," the huge knight said quietly, "in just a few moments your father is going to risk his life for you, and I hope that you will realize that this is the result of his great love for you. He would gladly give his life for you, but I will be present to make certain that doesn't happen."

He turned and looked deeply into Joel's eyes. "Your father is going to ask you to do something that you will find absolutely terrifying, yet you must obey him without a moment's hesitation. Do you understand what I am saying?"

Joel nodded. "Aye, sir." He studied the man's face. "Who are you, sire? How do you know my name?"

The big man hesitated. "I am Tertius. I was sent because of King Emmanuel's great love for you."

Joel glanced down at a deep rut in the road as he stepped around it. "How do you know—" The words died on his lips as he stared in astonishment. The tall soldier had vanished.

Bitter tears stung his eyes as he thought about the man's words. *Everything that he said was true,* he told himself. *I am here because of my own foolishness. Oh, that I had listened to Pa instead of Lank and the others whom I thought would be my friends!*

He brushed away the tears and swallowed hard. *Oh, that I could have but one more chance! If I could somehow make it back home to Seawell, I would strive to be as loyal to my father as he has been to me.* He sighed deeply. *But perhaps that chance will never come.*

"Lad, are you going to the Festival?" A friendly voice interrupted his thoughts and he looked up to see a bearded nobleman astride a tall, dark horse. The animal was so close that Joel could have reached out and touched it. The rider wore a royal blue doublet with gold beading, blue and gold trunk hose, and a cloak of deep blue about his shoulders. His hands were large and rough, the hands of a laborer, not those of a nobleman.

"Aye, sire, I am going to the Festival," Joel replied, and his heart pounded madly.

"Seawell is waiting, lad," the man said.

Joel looked up into his father's eyes and suddenly realized that this was the critical moment. He began to tremble with anticipation.

"Step behind my horse, lad," Cobby said in a low voice, "and then leap up and hook your chain over the pommel of the saddle. Keep your feet high."

"You there, sire," a soldier called out to Cobby. "Ride on, if you please, sire, and don't interfere with our slaves."

Cobby looked at the soldier. "Aye, sir. I'll ride on, sir." And then to his son, "Ready, go!"

Joel stepped behind his father's horse and then leaped forward, thrusting his manacled hands upward to catch his chain on the saddle pommel. The horse shot forward like a bolt from a crossbow, jerking Joel painfully forward. He remembered to bend his knees, lifting his feet to keep them clear of the pounding hooves. His father's strong right hand gripped his upper arm in a firm hold.

"Stop!" an authoritative voice shouted. "Runaway slave! Stop them!"

The galloping horse thundered down a slope and into the forest, darting at full speed between the trees in a desperate dash for freedom. Cobby and Joel both knew that capture would mean immediate death for both of them. "Are you all right, Son?"

Joel nodded. "Aye," he grunted.

"We have only two furlongs to ride, so listen closely," Cobby told him. "Do you have your harness in place?"

Joel grunted painfully. "Aye."

"As soon as I stop the horse, leap down and I will pull the hook out the top of your tunic. I have strung a line with a pulley on it across the canyon. Both are from the *Princess*. Your hook and mine will go into a large ring hanging below the pulley. Together we will ride the pulley across the canyon."

Joel's heart constricted with fear. "Pa, I can't!"

"It's the only way, Son," Cobby replied breathlessly. "Once we cross the canyon, we will be beyond the reach of our pursuers. It will take them at least three minutes to cross the bridge and come back to our landing point."

"Pa," Joel said plaintively, "I can't!" At that instant, Tertius' words seemed to ring in his ears. *"Your father is going to ask you to do something that you will find absolutely terrifying, yet you must obey him without a moment's hesitation."*

Twisting around to look back over his shoulder, Joel saw two mounted knights thundering through the woods about fifty yards behind them. At that moment, the lead horse stumbled and went down and the second horse crashed into it, throwing both riders to the ground. Unseen by Joel, a huge, blond warrior leaped upward, soaring above the trees.

"This is it, Son," Cobby called, reining the powerful black

to an abrupt halt at the very brink of the canyon. "Please trust me in this."

He leaped from the back of the horse as Joel jerked his hands free of the saddle and tumbled backwards to the ground. Cobby was upon him in an instant, ripping the gaudy surcoat apart and then reaching a strong hand down inside the front of his tunic to pull out the line and the hook. "On your feet, Son!" he cried.

As Joel leaped to his feet, he saw three or four mounted knights charging through the trees. His father lifted both hands, simultaneously thrusting the two hooks into an iron ring hanging just above their heads. "Ready, Son?" he called. "Lift your feet!"

"No, Pa!" Joel cried in terror, but Cobby had already thrown his weight forward, flinging them both over the edge of the canyon and out into empty space. Their combined weight hit the pulley and the line went taut, bouncing under the impact.

At that instant, a heavy battleaxe hurtled end over end across the canyon. The razor-sharp blade buried itself in the trunk of a sturdy oak, severing the line that was anchored to it. With cries of terror, Cobby and Joel fell into the emptiness of the abyss.

Chapter Seventeen

The battleaxe severed the line at the very point where Cobby had secured it to a sturdy oak. Together, in one horrifying, heart-stopping moment, father and son fell into the canyon, hurtling toward the rocky stream three hundred feet below.

The line abruptly tightened and the pulley screamed as it whirred along the line, carrying Cobby and Joel with it. Both looked up in astonishment to see a huge, powerful warrior standing at the far edge of the canyon, holding the end of the line in his muscular hands. In an instant they both landed on the rocky ledge beside him and he released the line and grabbed them to keep them from toppling back into the canyon.

Joel stared at the warrior. "Tertius!"

Cobby looked from one to the other. "Do you know each other?"

Joel continued to stare. "You caught the end of the line to keep us from falling? That's impossible! No one could be that fast or that strong."

"We have no time for talk, my friends," Tertius said urgently. "Even now they seek to destroy you." At these words, a bolt from a crossbow thudded into a tree beside them. Cobby and

Joel looked across the canyon to see three of Lord Tarak's soldiers crouching at the edge of the canyon. One raised a longbow and released an arrow. Cobby leaped in front of Joel and the arrow buried itself in Cobby's forearm.

Tertius hurled an enormous log across the canyon, striking all three knights and knocking them backwards to the ground. "Let's go," he said. "Grab my shoulders and hang on tightly!" Cobby and Joel both reached up and wrapped their arms around the massive shoulders. To their astonishment, the enormous warrior climbed straight up the rock face, carrying the two with him. When he reached level ground he hurried into the trees and then set his two burdens down.

"There is a cave where I have a cache of supplies," Cobby told him, grimacing in pain as he clutched the arrow. "I have a hammer and chisel with which to remove Joel's shackles."

"That is where I am taking you," the huge knight replied, "but we need to remove Joel's shackles now so that he can move faster." Reaching down, he grasped the shackle on Joel's left wrist and in one quick movement snapped the iron, freeing Joel's hand. He repeated the action and removed the shackle from his right wrist. Joel and Cobby stared at Tertius in astonishment.

"Let's tend to that wound," the big man then told Cobby. He grasped Cobby's arm and gently withdrew the arrow. Blood spurted from the wound. Tertius wrapped his big fingers around Cobby's arm, applying pressure to the wound to stop the bleeding. Plucking a bright yellow leaf from a nearby bush, he placed it over the wound and held it firmly in place. When he removed his hand a moment later, the bleeding had stopped completely.

"Let's go," Tertius urged. "Your adversaries will be here in just a few moments." Parting the branches of a thicket behind them, he revealed a trail and then indicated with a nod of his head that they were to follow it. Cobby and Joel darted through the opening and dashed down the trail.

"This way," Tertius called a moment later. Father and son turned as one to see their guide beckoning to them from a side trail that they had just passed. They followed him and he led them through the forest, down through a narrow, rocky ravine and then up a steep slope. At last he paused at a narrow fissure in the rocky hillside. "Your cave, sir," he said to Cobby. "Stay here for one hour until the search for you dies down."

"This was a shorter route than what I had chosen," Cobby told him.

Tertius nodded and then pointed. "When you leave, take that trail to the right, for it will lead you back to the bridge. Your pursuers will never find you here, but I will stand guard to be certain." With these words, he vanished.

Joel followed his father through the crevice in the rock and entered a narrow cavern. "I have a change of clothes for each of us," Cobby explained, leading Joel to a dim corner of the cavern. "There's not much I can do to disguise your height, but I can at least change your appearance somewhat and cover that flaming red hair of yours. Try these on." He handed Joel some items of clothing.

Joel accepted the clothing but stood looking at his father. "Pa," he said quietly, "you took an arrow for me. Back there at the canyon, you jumped in front of me to take an arrow that was intended for me. You saved my life!"

Cobby shrugged. "You're my son." He glanced at the wound in his arm. "I'd do it again if I needed to."

"Was the horse yours?"

Cobby stared at him. "The horse?"

"The black was one magnificent horse, Pa, yet you left her

at the canyon for Lord Tarak's men to take. Was she yours?"

"Aye, well, she was mine for three days. I bought her in Corthia."

"Pa, a horse like that would cost a fortune, yet you left her behind as if she didn't even matter. You traded her for my freedom."

His father sighed. "It was a fair trade, Son. I'd do it again in a heartbeat."

"I know you would, Pa, but where did you get the money? I know that was one expensive horse and I know that you don't have that kind of money. Where did it come from? And the clothes—regal clothing like that would cost a fortune. Where did the money come from?"

Cobby looked uncomfortable. "We'll talk about that later, Son. Right now the main objective is to get you home safely."

"Why didn't you just try to buy me back from Lord Tarak?" Joel persisted. "Wouldn't that have been easier?"

His father shook his head. "I learned that Corthian law prohibits the sale of any slave except in the slave markets. The penalties for breaking that law are fierce. It would have been pointless to try to talk Lord Tarak into selling you."

Overcome with emotion, Joel threw his arms around his father. "Thank you, Pa. I know this trip cost you dearly, and it nearly cost you your life. I guess I never realized how much you loved me."

Cobby embraced him. "If we can get you home safely, it will be worth everything."

"How did you get to Corthia, Pa?"

"We sailed the *Princess* here, of course."

"We?"

"Papa Wynn and I. He's guarding the boat right now."

"How did you string the line across the canyon?"

His father laughed. "You could figure that one out, Son. I simply tied a cord to an arrow and fired it across, and then tied the heavier line to the cord. I crossed at the bridge, hiked back to the arrow, and then pulled the line across to me."

"Did you actually ride the pulley across to test it?"

"Three times," Cobby replied. "It worked beautifully each time."

"Thank you, Pa," Joel said quietly. "Thank you for everything you did for me. I only regret that I put you through all this."

Cobby nodded. "Try the clothes on, Son."

Two minutes later, father and son stood side by side, outfitted from head to toe in brown and forest green. Each clutched a well-worn hunting bow. Joel adjusted his hat and turned to his father. "Well, Pa, do I look the part of a huntsman?"

Cobby chuckled. "I believe you do, Son. I hope we both do, at least enough to fool anyone who might still be looking for us."

Hours later, footsore and hungry, Joel and Cobby plodded wearily down a wide, noisy boulevard. The stalls of traveling merchants lined both sides of the street and the delicious smells of hot pies, spiced wines and gingerbread wafted through the air. Women admired fine woolen cloth woven in Akbran and gazed longingly at soft gloves and slippers crafted by skillful leatherworkers in Napis. Young men gazed eagerly at ornate swords and daggers from Karmany and Euristan, while young women marveled at the beautiful silks and brocades from East Terrestria. Musicians, jugglers, acrobats and even trained animals performed in the street to the delight of scores of young children.

Thousands of drunken revelers staggered in the streets or engaged in frivolous activities, and the local pickpockets and petty thieves plied their trade. Other townspeople swapped stories and caught up on news and gossip. Intent on reaching the waterfront, Joel and Cobby had to weave their way through the noisy, festive mob.

"Unless I'm mistaken," Cobby told Joel, "we're less than a mile from the waterfront. It's less than an hour till sunset, so we made good time, lad."

"Will Papa Wynn be waiting for us with the *Princess?*" Joel asked.

"He's out in the bay on the *Princess*," Cobby replied. "He'll sail in when I signal him. We can't tie up at the piers without an expensive license from the Port Authority."

"How is your arm, Pa?"

"It still throbs with pain," Cobby admitted, "but I think it will be all right."

"Excuse me, sire," Joel said to a drunken nobleman, attempting to step around him as he tried to keep pace with his father. The man stepped backwards, stumbling into Joel in the process and spilling rum all over him.

Joel hurried away from. "I smell like I've been drinking, Pa," he said in disgust, as his mind associated the smell of the rum with his captivity.

"May this be the only time you smell this way, Son," Cobby replied.

As they neared the waterfront, Cobby turned into a narrow alley. "There's one thing we must do before we signal the *Princess* and sail for home," he told Joel. "Not far from here are a score of men who will die unless we come to their rescue." He rummaged under a pile of weathered, rotting lumber and pulled out a coil of rope. "The seine line from the *Princess*," he explained to Joel. "We'll use it to free a number of men who I believe are innocent."

Shouldering the coil of line, he led Joel to a small court-yard overlooking the bay. He carefully scanned the courtyard to make sure that he was not being watched and then dropped the coil of rope on the flagstones beside a yawning black hole nearly three feet in diameter. As Joel watched in bewilder-ment, Cobby tied one end of the line to the upright of a hitch-ing post and then lowered the line into the hole. At that point Joel noticed that four knotted loops had been tied near the end of the line.

Cobby then lay down at the edge of the hole and peered into the darkness below. Cupping his hands to his mouth, he called softly, "Levi, are you there?"

"I am, but who are you?" a startled voice answered from down below.

"It is I, Cobby of Seawell. I did find a way out of mortis vivus. I have returned to help you get out as well." As these words were spoken, a chorus of voices echoed from down below, some calling Cobby's name, others pleading for help.

"Levi, help the men onto the rope one at a time. There are loops at the very end in which they can place their feet. My son and I will pull them up one by one until all of you are free."

"Bless you, Cobby!" came the grateful reply from down be-low. "May your children and grandchildren prosper and may your name be revered forever."

Cobby and Joel worked together, pulling the emaciated men one by one from the loathsome dungeon until all were free, though it took nearly half an hour. Some of the men broke into tears as they reached the surface and saw daylight; others tried to hug their benefactors. "Move away quickly and lose yourself in the city," Cobby curtly told each man. "If the soldiers come, we are all dead men."

Joel watched as prisoner after prisoner expressed his

gratitude to Cobby when he was released, calling him by name and thanking him profusely. At last, Joel's curiosity got the best of him and he had to ask. "How do these men know you, Pa?"

"I was a prisoner in this wretched place, but only briefly," Cobby replied, pulling on the rope to bring the next man up.

"How did you get out?"

"There's an underground stream that flows through the bottom. I swam out by following the stream."

"Then why didn't these men go out the same way? Why did they just stay here?"

Cobby hesitated. "There was no way of knowing if the stream was the way out," he said finally. "We didn't know if the water ever made its way to the surface or if it simply flowed into the heart of Terrestria and never again saw daylight."

"If the stream never surfaced, you would have drowned," Joel said thoughtfully.

Cobby nodded. "It was a risk that I had to take."

"But why, Pa? Why did you do it? You took a huge chance."

"I had to," Cobby said simply. "I couldn't stay in that hole day after day, knowing that you were in chains somewhere, and that I was the only one who could help free you."

Joel thought about it for a moment as the next prisoner reached the surface and did a jig when he was knew that he was free. "Thank you, thank you, Cobby of Seawell. I owe my life to you." Throwing his hands into the air to celebrate his freedom, the man hurried across the courtyard and disappeared around the corner.

"How far did you swim?" Joel asked.

Cobby shrugged and then laughed. "I was under so long that I just knew I was not going to make it. Just when I couldn't hold my breath any longer and knew that I was going to die, the stream came out on the hillside just above the bay. Was I glad to see daylight!"

"How many times have you risked your life for me on this trip?"

Cobby shook his head and didn't reply.

At last, father and son worked together to pull up the last prisoner, Levi. The man burst into tears when they pulled him from the hole. "Bless you, Cobby, bless you," he sobbed, kneeling at Cobby's feet and clutching his tunic. "I never expected to escape from mortis vivus. May King Emmanuel himself reward you."

Cobby embraced the man. "Go quickly," he urged. "A new life awaits you, but you must go before the soldiers discover what we have done."

At that moment, two guards rushed across the courtyard with drawn swords. "Stay where you are!" one cried. "Make one move and you're all dead men!"

Chapter Eighteen

Joel and Cobby looked up in horror as the burly soldiers raced across the courtyard with swords drawn. Levi leaped to his feet and dashed away, but the soldiers ignored him, intent on capturing Joel and Cobby. *We're so close to freedom!* Joel thought in desperation. *We shouldn't have stopped to help these men.*

Cobby sprang to his feet, and to Joel's amazement, held a gleaming sword in his right hand. With a snarl of rage the first soldier rushed Cobby, swinging his sword in a vicious cut intended to disembowel the fisherman. But Cobby merely sidestepped the blow, seized the assailant by the shoulder and hurled him forward, and kicked his legs from beneath him at the same time. With a cry of alarm the soldier plunged headfirst into the yawning hole in the ground and disappeared into the darkness of the dungeon below.

Cobby spun around, his sword ready for the next assault, but the second soldier was a bit more cautious. He advanced slowly, sword ready, watching Cobby warily. Joel scrambled to a safe vantage point behind his father.

"Give yourself up, peasant," the soldier snarled, circling slowly to the left. "Drop your sword or I'll end your life right now."

"That might be harder than you think, friend," Cobby replied calmly. "I'll make you the same offer: if you drop your sword, I won't have to end your life."

The soldier sneered. "What chance does a peasant huntsman have against a trained soldier? Your words will be your undoing, peasant, for I will take great delight in making your death as painful as possible rather than ending your life quickly."

"'Let not him that girdeth on his harness boast himself as he that putteth it off,'" Cobby replied, quoting a statement from Emmanuel's book. "You talk as if the outcome of the battle has already been decided in your favor. I warn you, friend, you won't find me that easy to kill."

Joel stared at his father, for he showed not the slightest trace of fear, though he was facing possible death at the hands of an armed soldier. *Pa is absolutely fearless,* he told himself in astonishment.

"Then prepare to die, peasant," the man growled, "for you will not leave this courtyard alive." With these words he charged Cobby, and his sword was quick, but his movements were precise and expected and Cobby's sword met each attack effortlessly. A cut, a series of lightning-quick slices, a flawlessly executed combination—the exasperated soldier tried every move he knew to get past the calm defenses of this troublesome peasant, yet Cobby met and repelled each advance. The fisherman stayed on the defensive, fending off each attack yet not pressing a counterattack of his own. Joel began to wonder why.

Within moments the soldier was panting with exertion, while Cobby remained calm but ready, and Joel began to grasp his father's strategy. Poised and confident, Cobby was simply allowing his adversary to wear himself out. A wild, desperate look had appeared in the soldier's eyes and he paused to wipe the sweat from his face. Screaming with rage, he lunged at Cobby with a vicious thrust of the deadly sword.

Cobby parried the thrust and countered with a cut, opening a gash in the soldier's sword arm. The man's eyes grew wide as if he had not even considered such a possibility. With a snarl of rage he advanced on Cobby, gasping for breath as he bore down with every bit of strength he had left in a quick series of cuts and slices. Joel watched in awe as his father calmly met and deflected each assault. At last, when the desperate soldier overextended himself with an ill-timed thrust, Cobby opened a wound in his side.

The soldier dropped his sword and fell on his knees. "I yield, my good man. Spare my life, I beg you."

Cobby's expression never changed. "Step into the hole."

"What?"

"Step into the hole. I can't release you, for you would bring the others. Step into the hole."

The man's face paled. "That's the living death! I'll never get out alive."

Cobby raised his sword. "It's either that or the sword. Which will it be?"

The man stepped into the hole and disappeared from sight.

Cobby turned to Joel. "Well, Son, let's go home. We need to get to the docks and signal Papa Wynn." Together they hurried from the courtyard.

"That was a very unselfish thing to do, Pa," Joel said, "stopping to rescue those poor wretches. Most of them looked as if they are in the final stages of death, yet now you have given them hope. Who were they? Why were they in the dungeon?"

"Most of them were honest men," Cobby replied, "thrown into the dungeon because they offended the wrong people in this vile city. Perhaps we released a few men that should not have been, but I don't think there's a man among them who received a fair trial. I couldn't just let them rot down there, knowing that most of them were innocent."

Moments later they reached the waterfront and hurried along the wharves, eager to signal Papa Wynn and sail for home. The waterfront was deserted, as nearly everyone in Corthia was at the Festival. "There's the *Princess* now," Cobby told Joel, pointing across the bay to a lone fishing vessel out on the open sea.

"She's quite a sight, Pa," Joel replied, and then choked up.

"Let's go home, Son."

Cobby climbed the slope just above the harbor. As Joel watched from the wharf down below, his father removed his cloak and began to wave it furiously, then held it overhead and ran along the brink of the hill with it. Joel turned and gazed across the bay in time to see the *Princess'* sail being hoisted.

"He saw you, Pa," Joel called. "Papa Wynn saw your signal."

As they watched, the *Princess* turned her bow and bounded eagerly toward the Corthian harbor. Joel trembled with excitement as the cog glided into the watercourse and headed eagerly for the wharf where Joel and his father stood. The sail came tumbling down as Papa Wynn released it and then scrambled for the tiller once again. The *Princess* glided to a stop and sat gently rocking in the swells some twenty yards from the wharf.

Papa Wynn was embarrassed. "Sorry. I just don't do it as well as you, Cobby. I guess I'm just a mite too cautious." He walked forward. "Let me break out the oars."

"Throw us a line, Pa," Cobby called. "Joel and I will pull you in."

Two minutes later, the *Princess* nudged against the dock. Joel and Cobby scrambled down the ladder and leaped aboard. Papa Wynn grabbed Joel and embraced him for a long moment. "I never thought I'd see you again, Son. Praise His Majesty, you're still alive!" As Papa Wynn released him, Joel saw that the old man's eyes were wet with tears.

Cobby was already breaking out the oars. "Let's get out of here as fast as possible, Pa, and put as many miles between us and Corthia as we possibly can tonight. I'm sure that Joel doesn't want to spend another moment here."

Moments later the *Princess* glided out into the open sea with Papa Wynn at the tiller. A westerly wind filled her sail and she bounded forward eagerly as though she knew that she was headed home. The wind hummed in the rigging and the sail snapped and popped as the ship's mast creaked and groaned. Salt spray splashed over the port gunwale, and the mist drifted across Joel, wetting his face. He took a deep breath and suddenly realized how much he had missed the exhilarating freedom of the vast open sea.

He turned and looked back at the city, and a tremendous sense of satisfaction rose in his breast as he watched the magnificent skyline recede and then grow smaller and smaller. *Free at last!* he thought gratefully. *Never again will I see Corthia! Never again will I see Chamac, or Lord Tarak. Never again will I see Vardaman's sneering face, or hear his hateful voice. I'm free of the overseers, free of the leg irons. I'm really free!*

His thoughts turned to Micah and he felt a cold, empty sorrow deep within. *He died as a slave in a hostile land,* he told himself mournfully. *What a lonely, miserable way to go. He'll never see his home and family again.*

He thought of Myra, and his throat tightened. His heart seemed to constrict within him. *Somewhere in that wretched city, Myra is still a slave. She still wears wrist irons. Tonight she'll sleep somewhere in the street, chained to a score of other slaves, and tomorrow she'll wake up, still chained, still a slave.* His eyes welled with tears. *Oh, Myra, Myra.*

He felt a hand on his shoulder and turned to see his father's eyes filled with tears. "Your thoughts are troubled, Son. What's on your mind?"

Joel swallowed hard, and for a long moment, found that he couldn't even speak.

Cobby squeezed his shoulder and waited. "It's all right, Son."

"I—I was thinking about Micah and Myra," Joel replied at last. "Micah is dead, and Myra is still a slave to Belosi." Briefly, he told the details of Micah's death at the hands of the overseer. "I just knew him a few weeks, Pa, for I just met him on the slave galley, but he was a friend. He was the only friend I had in Corthia."

His father nodded. "I'm sorry, Son." He cleared his throat. "Who was Myra?"

"Myra was from Seawell. She was the tinsmith's daughter, I think. I didn't know her well, but I liked her, and I think she liked me." He blinked back new tears. "She's still a slave, Pa. Can't we do something?"

Pa took a deep breath. "I wouldn't know how to go about finding her, Son. Did she belong to Lord Tarak?"

"She belonged to Lord Tarak's son, Belosi, on the estate next to ours."

"I wouldn't know where to even find her."

"You found me, Pa."

Cobby nodded. "All praise to Emmanuel. Aye, with his guidance, I did. Perhaps her father will one day find and rescue her."

Joel turned to face him. "I don't know everything that you

and Papa Wynn went through to get here, Pa, and I don't know everything that you went through once you were here. But I do know enough to know that it wasn't easy, and I want you to know that I am deeply grateful for everything that you and Papa Wynn have done."

Cobby embraced him.

"Pa, I want to ask you something. That horse was magnificent, and I know she would have cost a fortune. I know that you and Papa Wynn just paid off the *Princess* and that you didn't have much saved. Pa, how did you pay for such an expensive horse?"

His father turned and looked across the waves, but didn't answer.

"Pa?"

"We'll talk of this later, Son. Perhaps when we reach Seawell."

Joel nodded. "As you wish, Pa."

He turned and looked astern. The city of Corthia was barely visible in the distance. At that moment, the reality of his freedom sank in, and it was as if a crushing weight abruptly lifted from his shoulders. He was no longer a slave and he was beyond the reach of Vardaman and Lord Tarak.

He took a deep breath of the sea air. "Someday, Pa," he said quietly, "I wish someone could return to Corthia and rescue Myra."

Papa Wynn called from the tiller, "Son, we're losing daylight fast. Do you want to find a place to harbor for the night?"

"Nay," Cobby replied, without even pausing to consider the matter. "We want to put as many miles as possible between us and Corthia. Stay in sight of land, but keep sailing. Perhaps His Majesty will smile on us and we will have a clear night."

The stars began to appear one by one in a platinum sky. The

night was clear and cool, and the moon that slowly rose over the stern was nearly full, etching the crest of each wave with silver light and brightening the sea so that sailing was possible. Eager to get home to Seawell, the three travelers sailed through the night, taking turns as helmsman and bow lookout while the third person slept.

When the rising sun painted the eastern sky with brilliant hues of mauve and gold, Wynn took the tiller from Cobby. "I'd say we've come seventy miles."

Cobby nodded. "We've made good time."

Joel rose from his pallet beside the mast, yawning and stretching as he joined the two men in the stern. "We've come quite a way, haven't we?"

"Aye," his father responded, "quite a way."

"Last night we had a good, brisk wind behind us the entire time that I was at the tiller," Joel said, "and it seemed that we were making excellent time. The *Princess* seemed to know that she was going home, and she was almost flying!"

The men laughed.

"I'm ready for breakfast," Papa Wynn said, opening a tin of hardtack. "Will you gentlemen join me?" After sending a petition of thanksgiving to King Emmanuel, the men sat down to eat while Joel took the helm, holding the tiller with one hand and his piece of hardtack with the other.

"Pa," Joel said between bites, "at the courtyard you went against two trained knights, yet you easily defeated both of them. You fought like a master swordsman. Were you ever a knight?"

Cobby smiled. "I've been a fisherman all my life, Son."

"Then where did you learn to fight like that? You handle the sword like a master swordsman."

The men exchanged glances. "Actually, Joel, your grandfather taught me. Any skills I have, I learned from him."

"You fought like a master!" Joel said again.

Cobby shrugged. "I had the sword of Emmanuel. It's invincible."

"Would you teach me to use the sword like that?"

"Actually, Joel, I was planning to do just that. Papa Wynn and I were talking about it this morning. The use of the sword is not for the knight alone. I should have taught you long ago—that's one area in which I have failed you."

"When?" Joel persisted.

"There's no time like the present," Cobby replied. "The *Princess* won't reach Seawell for at least a fortnight. That will give us plenty of time to teach you the basics."

And so the lessons in swordsmanship began right after breakfast. With Papa Wynn at the tiller, Cobby began to instruct his son in the proper use of the sword. They cleared an area just forward of the mast to use as a training stage and then Cobby got out two swords and the training commenced.

"The first thing you must know," Cobby told Joel, "is how to defend yourself in the event of an attack. First and foremost, the sword is used for defense. Learning how to stage a good defense is as important as learning how to attack."

"Yesterday in the courtyard, in the battle against the two knights, your defense was magnificent," Joel replied. "They did most of the fighting, yet you defeated them both."

"The victory is Emmanuel's and the credit is his," Cobby replied earnestly. "The first soldier was slow and clumsy, and he attacked without knowing what he was up against. The second was far more skilled, yet his movements were predictable and it was easy to anticipate every move before he made it."

Joel frowned. "How?"

"I watched his eyes and I watched his feet."

"His eyes and his feet?"

"Aye. His feet told me what he was going to do and his eyes told me when. If you know what your opponent is going to do before he does it, you can anticipate his attack and have your defense strategy in place."

"I noticed that you didn't press an attack for the first few minutes," Joel remarked. "You just defended yourself while he attacked you."

"You saw what happened, didn't you? I simply allowed him to wear himself out and then when his energy was spent and his reflexes were slow, I counterattacked."

Joel laughed. "It worked."

Cobby nodded. "Raise your sword. Let me show you how to stand when you are anticipating an assault."

For the next several days, the hull of the *Princess* was the scene of one fierce battle after another as Joel's training progressed. Cobby and Papa Wynn both took part in the instruction, as both were master swordsmen. Over and over they stressed the fact that strength in battle came from King Emmanuel himself, and that victory came only as one learned to battle in this strength.

Joel applied himself during the exercises, watching Pa's every move with the sword, studying his footwork, noting how and when he choose to advance and when he decided to retreat. He recognized that both his father and grandfather were master swordsmen and he wisely set out to learn everything he could from them.

They taught him how to study his opponent and know how to anticipate his moves, how to defend himself against any attack, and how and when to counterattack. Joel was an apt pupil and learned quickly.

One afternoon, as Joel and Cobby were sparring, Papa

186

Wynn stood at the tiller, guiding the ship and watching the exchange. "He's doing well, isn't he, Son?" he commented, addressing Cobby.

"That he is, Pa," Cobby agreed. He wiped the sweat from his brow. "His footwork is good—well, as good as one could expect aboard a tossing ship—and he pays close attention to what his opponent is planning. His reflexes are fantastic. He's as quick as a hummingbird. With a little more practice and a bit of experience, he'll make an excellent swordsman. I just wish..." Cobby paused and let out a long sigh.

Papa Wynn noticed. "What's wrong?"

"I just wish that I had trained my son properly," he replied. "Had Joel been trained in the use of the sword before the Dragon Tournament, he never would have been taken captive and been sold as a slave in Corthia." He looked at Joel. "I'm sorry, Son. I failed you."

"If I had been wise enough to listen to you," Joel countered, "I never would have gone to the Tournament in the first place."

Papa Wynn lashed the tiller in place and went to one of the water barrels for a drink. "We had better put ashore soon," he said to Cobby.

"Why, Pa? What's wrong?"

"We're out of water," the old man replied. "We need to stop and take on a fresh supply."

Cobby nodded. "Move in closer to shore," he suggested. "We'll watch for a stream or a river."

Papa Wynn brought the *Princess* in closer to shore and all three passengers began to watch for a source of fresh water. They had sailed just another mile or two when Joel spotted a small river flowing into a picturesque bay bordered with white sands. "There, Papa Wynn," he called. "We can put in there."

THE ISLE OF DRAGONS

Moments later the *Princess* glided into the bay as Cobby dropped the sail. Joel readied the oars. With Papa Wynn at the tiller, Cobby and Joel rowed the cog into the mouth of the river. Joel lowered a bucket over the starboard gunwale at the end of a line and pulled up a bucketful of fresh water, which he then emptied into the water barrel. Cobby worked at the port rail with a second bucket. Within five minutes they had filled one water barrel and were working on the second. "Just a few more, boys, and we'll be on our way," Papa Wynn called.

"Just another bucket or two should do it," Cobby said, flinging his bucket over the side again, "and then we'll—Arrgh!" He dropped his line and slapped furiously at his neck, dancing around frantically.

"What happened?" Papa Wynn asked, with a puzzled look on his face.

"A wasp got me!" Cobby yelped. "He stung me twice on the neck." He glanced at the timbers beneath his feet where a large, yellow-black insect lay, buzzing and turning in slow circles. "It's a hornet," he exclaimed. "Look at the size of that thing!" He stepped on the hornet, crushing it beneath his boot.

"You dropped your bucket, Pa," Joel said, pointing to the wooden bucket, which was now floating downstream. "I'll get it for you." Stripping off his shoes and tunic, he jumped overboard and swam after the errant bucket. He retrieved it and stood in the shallows near the riverbank.

"After two weeks at sea, it's good to be on solid ground," he called to the others. "Pa, I'm going to take a quick look around." Stepping from the water, he climbed up the riverbank, carrying the bucket.

Two men rose from the bushes, seized the startled youth by the arms, and pulled him down into a thicket. A dirty hand was clapped over his mouth before he could utter a sound.

Chapter Nineteen

Cobby turned just in time to see Joel disappear into the bushes bordering the riverbank. "Joel," he called, "what happened?"

Joel struggled desperately against the two men who held him. Writhing like a fish out of water, he managed to jerk his right arm free. He whirled and threw his entire weight against the other man, knocking him off balance. Both he and his captor tumbled forward and slid down the steep bank, landing on the gravel bar at the edge of the water.

With a roar of rage, Cobby seized the bow anchor and hurled it overboard, then grabbed two swords and leaped into the water. He splashed ashore with a sword in each hand to find both of Joel's assailants ready with swords drawn. Dashing to Joel's side, he tossed him a sword and then turned to face the enemy. "This is what you trained for, Son," he said in a low voice. "Stay close to me and together we'll see this through."

At that moment, four more armed men appeared on the bank above them. Papa Wynn hit the water with a sword in his hand. "Six of them, three of us," he called to Cobby and Joel, "but we battle with King Emmanuel's sword, so the victory is ours."

Just as Papa Wynn splashed ashore, the four bandits charged down the bank and swords clashed as the battle was joined. A tall bandit leaped at Joel, swinging his sword in a furious overhand cut which Joel anticipated and met with his own blade. He felt the impact of steel against steel through the hilt of his sword.

"Well done, Son," Cobby called, though he was battling two adversaries. "Anticipate what he is going to do and then defend against it. Wait for the right moment and then counterattack." His sword flew as he stood firm against a relentless attack by two swords simultaneously.

The clearing rang with the sounds of the conflict as the three travelers defended themselves against the six attackers. Papa Wynn managed to reach Joel and Cobby and the three stood side by side as they battled for their lives. Struggling to hold his own against a more experienced swordsman, Joel found to his amazement that somehow he was not afraid. The presence of his father and grandfather brought a measure of strength and courage.

Cobby caught the blade of one of his adversaries with his own blade and sent the weapon flying into the river, leaving the attacker defenseless. With one clean stroke he ended the man's life.

Powerful hands suddenly seized Joel's sword hand, ripping the weapon from his grasp and pinning his arms behind him, rendering him helpless. Another attacker drew back his sword, preparing to end Joel's life. "Pa!" Joel screamed in desperation.

Papa Wynn leaped forward, raising his sword to defend Joel, but Joel's assailant grabbed his sword arm. Realizing that he could not free his sword in time to stop the fatal blow, Papa Wynn grabbed the sharp blade of the other man's sword with his bare hand, gashing it wide open. Blood poured from the wound. "Cobby!" he called.

With a cry of rage, Cobby bore down on the two assailants. His sword flew, forcing the two men to retreat before the fury of his attack. When he reached Papa Wynn and Joel he turned to his father. "How bad is your hand?"

"It's cut bad," Papa Wynn replied, clenching his injured hand in a tight fist to slow the bleeding, "but my sword hand is as good as ever! Let's finish this battle before we worry about the hand."

The five remaining assailants circled the three travelers and moved in to press the attack. "Fight in the power of King Emmanuel," Cobby reminded his companions, breathing hard. "The enemy is helpless before him."

Swords clashed as the five assailants charged in, screaming furiously as they sought to overcome the three travelers. Joel found himself facing a sturdy ruffian who swung his heavy sword with a vengeance. "I'll have your head, lad," he boasted with a wicked grin. "Your life is now measured in seconds."

"I bear the sword of King Emmanuel," Joel replied evenly. "Your defeat is already certain."

"Insolent lad," the man growled. "Prepare to die!" With these words he leaped at Joel, swinging his sword in a powerful horizontal cut.

Joel met the blow with his own blade, flinching as the heavy sword sent shock waves through his own. The assailant stepped back, took a deep breath, and launched a vicious assault, flying at Joel with a withering volley of cuts, slices and thrusts. Joel deftly foiled each attack, meeting steel with steel. When the man overextended himself with a hasty thrust, Joel saw an opening and inflicted a mortal wound to the man's torso. The man dropped his sword and stumbled backwards, clutching his side as he fell to the riverbank.

Joel turned and glanced at his father. Cobby's sword flew as he fought two assailants at the same time. At that moment, his sword ended the life of one attacker, and the other turned and fled up the riverbank.

Clenching his left fist to stem the bleeding, Papa Wynn fought the remaining two assailants. As Joel watched in astonishment, the old man's sword flew like lightning, slicing, parrying, and thrusting as he drove the men toward the bank. At last, both turned and fled.

Cobby let out his breath in a long sigh. "Well, I'm glad that's over." He glanced at Joel. "You all right, Son?"

Joel nodded. "I'm fine, Pa."

Cobby turned to Papa Wynn. "Let's take a look at that hand, Pa."

The old man opened his left hand and Joel winced when he saw the injury, a deep diagonal gash across the palm. Cobby grimaced and squeezed his father's wrist to stop the bleeding. "That's not good, Pa. You won't lose the hand, but you certainly will not have full use of it again."

He glanced at Joel. "Keep your sword ready, Son, while I tend to Papa Wynn's hand." Joel nodded.

Cobby scanned the clearing and then picked several dark-colored leaves from a nearby bush. Crushing the leaves in his fist, he then placed the crumpled fragments directly on the wound. He tore a long strip of cloth from the hem of his own jerkin and used it to bandage the wound, wrapping it tightly around the injured hand again and again. "There," he told his father with a note of satisfaction, "that should do it."

"Thank you, Son," Papa Wynn said quietly. "Now let's get out of here before more of these ruffians appear."

Cobby nodded. "Exactly."

Moments later, with Cobby and Joel at the oars, the *Princess* glided out across the bay toward the sparkling blue sea. Joel took the tiller, Cobby hoisted the sail, and the vessel almost seemed to leap forward as the wind filled the sail. "What were they after, Pa?" Joel asked. "Why did those men jump us?"

"I'm not sure," Cobby replied. "Perhaps they intended to rob us; or perhaps they hoped to steal the *Princess*. At any rate, whatever they were after, they failed in the attempt and we are all safe. Emmanuel's name be praised."

He looked at his father, who sat in the bow of the vessel. "How is your hand, Pa?"

"It hurts something fierce, Son, but I'll live."

"I'm sorry about your hand, Papa Wynn," Joel said contritely. "But for me, this would not have happened."

Three days later, two islands came into view off the port bow. Joel was forward at the time and he spotted them first. "The Twin Sisters!" he cried as he recognized the distant islands. "Pa, we're almost home! I can almost see Seawell from here. We're almost home!"

Cobby looked toward the Twin Sisters and an involuntary shudder passed over him as he viewed the islands. Painful memories surfaced, and he struggled to bury them in the depths of his subconscious.

Joel walked astern as he addressed his father and grandfather. "Thank you for what you have done for me on this trip. Thank you for risking your lives for my freedom. I don't know what all you went through on this trip, but I want you to know that I am grateful." He watched as the islands grew larger and larger. "I'm thankful that this trip is over. I sure wouldn't want to go through it again, but I guess all's well that ends well, aye?"

"Joel, there's something—" Cobby started to say, but Papa Wynn cut him off with a quick shake of the head. Had Joel seen the look that passed between the two men, he would have realized that there was far more to the story than what he knew and that the journey was far from being ended.

Chapter Twenty

The dragons roared. At that moment two gates slammed open and two dragons exploded into the arena. Terror swept over the young contender, rendering him unable to move, to breathe, or to think. The dragons were enormous, with massive bodies covered in gray scales, cavernous mouths with teeth like daggers, and claws that could rip through armor. Their long, scaly tails whipped back and forth like venomous serpents. Death had entered the arena.

The young contender glanced at his partners and saw to his amazement that all three of them, all older and more experienced than he, seemed eager to do battle with the monsters. He was terrified, and the pike trembled in his hands, but they seemed calm and unperturbed.

"Split up!" one contender called to the others. "Let's come at them from different directions!" Three of the youth scattered, leaving the youngest standing rooted to the spot, alone and vulnerable.

One dragon crept forward with a low growl rumbling in its throat. The massive head swept slowly from side to side. The huge golden eyes scanned the arena and then focused on the youngest contender. In horror the youth realized that the deadly beast had selected him as its prey. His heart pounded and his breath came in short, ragged gasps. The blood pounded in his head so loudly that he could no longer hear the roar of the crowd. His chest constricted and his limbs trembled. Overwhelmed with terror, he was paralyzed, unable to fight, unable to flee. The dragon opened his enormous mouth and filled the arena with an ear-shattering roar of rage.

Another contender dashed in front of the deadly beast, leaping high to slash at its throat with a glittering sword. The dragon snarled and swatted at the combatant, but then turned and continued to stalk his terrified prey.

"Don't just stand there!" another contender called to the terrified youth. "Run! Come on!" The older partner ran forward to engage the beast.

The youth ran after his partner, although his senses screamed for him to run in the other direction. His partner charged directly at the dragon and then at the last possible moment darted to one side, circling behind the creature. Bellowing with rage, the dragon turned to follow him.

The contender darted under the beast from behind, slashing upward at the great belly. The dragon dropped his head and seized his tormentor in his teeth, crushing the screaming youth and then with one quick movement of the massive head hurling the limp body twenty yards across the arena. The youngest contender stood rooted in the sand, staring in horror at the lifeless figure.

A scream reverberated across the arena, and he turned to see that the second dragon had pinned one of his partners beneath a huge, splayed foot. *The dragons are killing my partners one by one,* the youth thought desperately, *and soon I'll be facing both of them by myself!* An unexpected boldness swept over him and he ran forward to engage the dragon and rescue his partner.

He stabbed at the great golden eye, one of the beast's most vulnerable spots. The blow fell short and the point of the pike struck the fleshy part of the cheek, just below the eye. The beast flinched, roaring in pain, and the lad knew that he had found a tender spot. He leaped up again, striking the dragon again in the very same spot.

With a scream of fury that reverberated across the vast amphitheater like a crash of thunder, the great beast rolled away from the youth, freeing his partner in the process. The referees ran in with their blazing torches, driving the bellowing beast away from the downed contender, who scrambled to his feet, apparently unhurt. The referees backed off and the round resumed.

"I thank you," the older partner gasped. "He nearly killed me."

Both dragons came charging in at that moment and the battle continued. For the next fifteen seconds the two great beasts and the three remaining contenders gave the vast audience a performance they would never forget. Darting in and out, always circling the ponderous beasts, the youths managed to avoid the sharp claws and menacing jaws.

And then it happened. A dragon lunged for one of the contenders, and the youngest one leaped in, stabbing at the beast's great soft underbelly. But the youth had underestimated the dragon's cunning. The creature twisted to one side, swinging his mighty tail in a wide arc that slammed the youth against the rocky embankment. The pike went flying. In an instant the dragon was upon him, roaring in fury and slashing at him with his deadly claws. As the crowd roared with excitement, the hapless lad dropped to the sand and rolled beneath a ledge of rock.

The dragon bellowed and clawed at the ledge, determined

to get at the terrified contender. One huge foot raked the length of the ledge and a sharp claw slashed the side of the youth's leg, slicing his thigh open. He screamed in pain and drew his body as tight as he could against the back of the crevice. Roaring horribly, the furious dragon clawed at the ledge again and again. Dirt and rocks fell down upon the lad as the frenzied dragon dug at the ledge.

The young contender was terrified. *Where are my partners? Where are the referees?* He watched the deadly claws repeatedly pass within inches of his body. With each pass they came a little closer as the frenzied beast dug away at his hiding place. *Why don't the referees do something. . . .*

"Pa, what's wrong?" Joel's voice cut through Cobby's reverie, and the dragon and the arena disappeared in an instant. He blinked and realized that Joel stood staring at him intently. "Pa, what's wrong? You're crying."

Cobby took a deep breath before answering. "Joel, there's something I should have told you a long time ago. I should have warned you about the Dragon Tournament. How I wish I had."

"What's in the past is in the past," Papa Wynn said.

Cobby shook his head. "I think he needs to hear this, Pa." He looked at Joel. "Son, do you know why I walk with a limp? Do you know how my leg was injured?"

Joel nodded. "You were injured in battle, Pa. Your injury is a mark of courage."

Cobby shook his head. "It is true that I was injured in battle, but I never told you about the battle. I was injured by a dragon. Years ago, when I was just about your age, I was a contender in the Dragon Tournament. One of my partners was killed, and one of the dragons trapped me beneath a ledge at the side of the arena. The dragon tried to dig me out, and in doing so, slashed my leg badly. That's how I received my injuries."

Joel was speechless. He stared at his father as his mind struggled to accept what he was hearing. At last he found his voice. "The—the Dragon Tournament? But, Pa, that's impossible! The Tournaments didn't start until last year."

Cobby shook his head. "Nay, Son, there have always been Dragon Tournaments since the beginning of time. Our evil foe, Argamor, planned them, and wicked slavers like the Corthians have funded and developed them, all with the express purpose of capturing young slaves. Not always have the Tournaments been as elaborate as this one, but Argamor has always used dragons to draw hearts away from King Emmanuel. A few weeks ago a group of concerned fathers from Seawell went out to Elder Sister and destroyed the arena, but one day it will undoubtedly be rebuilt—perhaps in another location—and the Tournaments will resume."

He sighed. "It is quite possible that you fought the dragon that injured me." The tears rolled down his cheeks. "If only I had warned you. Somehow it never occurred to me that you would be drawn to the Tournament as I was."

"I fought a young dragon, Pa. It could not have been the same one."

"Dragons live for hundreds of years, Joel. A two-hundred-year-old dragon is a young one." Sobbing, he dropped his head. "Oh, my son, my son. If only I had warned you."

Papa Wynn stood at the tiller, steadily holding the *Princess* to her course.

Joel looked up to see the Seawell harbor approaching. "It's behind us, Pa," he said, as if to comfort his father. "I made a tragic mistake, but at least it's now behind us. We're home, Pa, home at last!"

He was stunned as the *Princess* continued past the harbor

entrance without turning in. "Papa Wynn," he called, "you missed the harbor. We passed it!"

His grandfather didn't answer.

Joel looked at his father. "Pa, what's going on?"

Cobby's face was grave. "We'll tell you shortly, Son."

"Are we going to Darwick?"

"Aye."

"But Pa, why aren't we going home? Why are we going to Darwick?"

Cobby took a deep breath, and Joel could tell that he was struggling with his emotions. "We're taking the *Princess* to her new owners."

Joel felt like a man just waking up from a bad dream to find that reality is as bad as the dream. His throat tightened. "What—what do you mean, Pa?"

Cobby sighed deeply, looked at Wynn, and then turned back to Joel. "You asked how I got the money to buy the mare we used in the escape at the canyon. Well, Son, you might as well know—the money came from the *Princess*. I sold her."

"You sold the *Princess*?" Joel was aghast. "But Pa, why? You love the *Princess*—why would you sell her?"

His father's lip was quivering. "I had to, Son. It—it was the only way I could raise the money to make the trip to rescue you. I sold her to the moneylenders for fifty percent of her actual value."

"Fifty percent? Why, Pa? Why would you sell her so cheap?" Like a beacon on a dark night, a ray of hope appeared as a sudden thought occurred. "Buy her back, Pa! Tell the moneylenders you'll buy her back. We can work together to pay off the loan again."

Cobby shook his head. "They've already told me that they won't sell her back to me, Son. The moneylenders only gave me fifty percent because they were taking a huge risk—they agreed to let me take the ship to Corthia in search of you."

"What would have happened if you hadn't brought the *Princess* back? What if you and Papa Wynn had been lost at sea?"

"They would have gotten our house. Your ma would have been widowed and homeless." Cobby sighed. "Son, she wanted me to go to Corthia to rescue you, even though she knew what it could cost her."

Joel was in agony as the *Princess* sailed into the harbor at Darwick. "Oh, Pa, I'm so sorry! Papa Wynn, I'm sorry! I wish I had never heard of the Dragon Tournament, for I had no way of knowing that it would cost our family so dearly!"

The setting sun painted the waters of the harbor with brilliant hues of mauve and crimson as the sail came tumbling down. The *Princess* glided to a mooring at the pier in front of the moneylenders. The long voyage was ended.

Author's Note

Today there are many dragons in our society, and youth are flocking to the Tournaments in record numbers. The dragons of pornography, immorality, rock music, drugs, alcohol, selfishness and rebellion are taking a tremendous toll on young people. Lives are being devastated.

Dragons are deadly. How often they destroy young lives, as they did the young contender in the story; and how often they lead youth into a slavery that's worse than death, as they did to Joel of Seawell. And yet, how many young people attend the Tournaments, daring to enter the arena with the dragons, never realizing that their lives and futures are at stake.

Avoid foolish friends. Mark any friend who offers you anything that will draw you away from the King or drive a wedge between you and your parents, and know that this person is not a true friend. Lank's only purpose in forming a friendship with Joel was to enslave him.

Learn to trust your parents. Almost without exception, your parents are the very best friends you will ever have in this life. As Tertius told Joel, one should strive to be as loyal to his parents as his parents are to him. If just one young person reads this book and realizes the wisdom of bonding with his or her parents and avoiding the deadly dragons of our treacherous society, it will have been worth every hour I spent in the writing of this book.

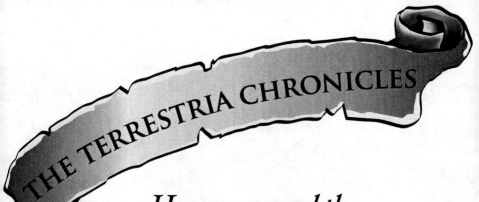